By the Same Author:

THE TIE THAT BINDS

WHERE

YOU

ONCE

BELONGED

A Novel

KENT HARUF

SUMMIT BOOKS
NEW YORK   LONDON   TORONTO
SYDNEY   TOKYO

Summit Books
Simon & Schuster Building
Rockefeller Center
1230 Avenue of the Americas
New York, New York 10020

Copyright © 1990 by Kent Haruf

DESIGNED BY BARBARA MARKS
Manufactured in the United States of America

10 9 8 7 6 5 4 3 2 1

Library of Congress Cataloging in Publication Data

Haruf, Kent.
    Where you once belonged: a novel / Kent Haruf.
        p.   cm.
    I Title.
PS3558.A716W48   1990
813' .54—dc20   89-37862
                                                     CIP

ISBN 0-671-65903-0

Part of this book was published in different form in
Grand Street and *Best American Short Stories 1987*.
It's a pleasure to acknowledge the generous support
given me by the Whiting Foundation.

·

For

three

Elizabeths:

Sorel,

Whitney,

and

Chaney

·

PART
ONE

ONE

In the end Jack Burdette came back to Holt after all. None of us expected it anymore. He had been gone for eight years and no one in Holt had heard anything about him in that time. The police themselves had stopped looking for him. They had traced his movements to California, but after he had entered Los Angeles they had lost him and finally they had given it up. Thus in the fall of 1985, so far as anyone in Holt knew, Burdette was still there. He was still in California and we had almost forgotten him.

Then late on a Saturday afternoon at the beginning of November he appeared in Holt once more.

He was driving a red Cadillac now. It was not a new car; he had bought it soon after he left town when he still had money to spend. Nevertheless it was still flashy, the kind of automobile you might expect a Denver pimp or a just-made oil millionaire in Casper, Wyoming, would drive. There was all that red paint—the color of a raw bruise, say, or the vivid smear of a woman's lipstick on a Saturday night—and all of it was shining, gleaming under the sun, looking as though he had spent an entire day polishing it for our benefit.

He drove this car, this affront and outrage to the entire town

if we had known in the beginning who was driving it, drove it
through Holt on Highway 34 and then turned around at the city
limits and came back and drove north up Main Street past the
water tower and the bank and the post office and the Holt
Theater, and finally parked it on Main Street in the middle of town
and didn't get out. Instead, for the rest of that afternoon and on
into the evening, he sat there as if he were waiting for something:
waiting and smoking cigarettes and spitting out through the
rolled-down side window onto the pavement and only now and
then shifting in the front seat to relieve the pressure of the steering
wheel against his gut. I suppose he thought someone in town
would say something to him. But no one did. Not at first. They
did not even seem to recognize him. For at least an hour his former
townsmen merely passed along in front of him, shopping, going
in and out of the stores on Saturday afternoon as usual, without
once stopping to speak or even to pause very long to look at the
Cadillac to see who owned it.

Eventually someone did think to call the sheriff, though. This
was Ralph Bird, who owns the Men's Store.

About four-thirty that afternoon Ralph Bird looked out
through the front display window of the Men's Store and noticed
the red Cadillac across the street in front of the tavern. He did
not think much about it at first. Pheasant season had begun and
there were strange vehicles in town anyway. Thirty minutes later,
though, when he looked across the street a second time he saw
that the car was still there, with the man he had seen earlier still
sitting alone in the front seat, and that bothered him. He began
to study the car. There was nothing familiar about it. But after
a minute or two he believed he detected something recognizable
about the man inside. He turned and called to his wife at the back
of the store.

"Hey," he said. "Come out here a minute."

"What do you want?"

·

"Come out here."

Hannah Bird came out from the storeroom where she'd been working among the ranks of wooden shelves. She was a tall thin woman with hair dyed a dark shade of red. She stood in the doorway brushing the hair out of her eyes. "What do you want?" she said. "I'm trying to get these shoe boxes put away."

"Look at this," Bird said.

"At what?"

"This car. See that guy inside?"

She walked to the front of the store. "I see him."

"What do you think about him?"

"I don't think anything about him."

"Keep looking."

She looked out through the display window again. Presently while she watched, the bloated-looking man in the front seat of the shiny car turned his head to spit and now she could see the side of his face. Hannah Bird recognized him at once.

"Now don't you do anything, Ralph," she said. "You leave that man alone."

"Sure," Bird said. "I thought it was him."

"But don't you bother him. You don't have any idea what that man might do."

"He still owes me money."

"I don't care. You let the police handle this."

Ralph Bird didn't listen to her. His wife put her hand on his arm as if she meant to control him, to hold him there by force, but he brushed her hand away as though it were no more than store lint. He opened the door and stepped outside.

"Ralph," she cried. "Ralph. You come back here, Ralph."

Along the street it had begun to grow chill and raw. The mercury lights had come on at the street corners and there was a little breeze starting up along the pavement. Bird looked up and down Main Street; it was nearly empty of people; then he stepped off the curb and crossed the street toward Burdette's red Cadillac. When he reached it he stopped for a moment to study the plates. The plates showed that the car had been licensed in California. Then he moved along the side toward the driver's door. He peered in. Burdette was staring back at him through the open window.

But Burdette looked bad now. In the eight years since Bird or any one of us had seen him he'd changed for the worse. He was fat now, obese; he was sloppy and excessive; his head had grown bald and the flesh hung on him like suet. "It was like," Bird would say later, "like for eight years he'd been feeding on cream pie and pork steak and lately he hadn't fed at all." Still it was Jack Burdette.

"You son of a bitch," Bird said. "What are you doing back here?"

"That you, Bird?"

"Yeah. It's me."

"I seen you in the mirror. Only I had about decided you wasn't going to speak to me. I thought you just wanted to admire this car."

"I'll speak to you," Bird said. "I'll speak to Bud Sealy too."

Burdette stared at Bird, then he laughed once, loud, harsh. So his laugh hadn't changed at all; it was the same sudden explosion that everyone remembered.

"That's right," Bird told him. "Go ahead. Enjoy it. You still got a few minutes."

"Why's that? Because you already told Bud Sealy I was here?"

"No. Because I'm going to."

"Go ahead, then. I ain't going nowhere. And you can tell Bud—" Burdette seemed to think. He spat once more out the window into the street, this time onto the pavement at Bird's feet. "You can tell him I'm looking forward to seeing him."

"You son of a bitch," Bird said. "You goddamn—"

Then abruptly Ralph Bird stopped talking. He moved away from the car and began to walk up the street toward the corner. He turned once and looked back, then he began to trot. By the time he reached the corner he was running. At Second Street he turned and ran east toward the courthouse a block away. He ran on, his arms pumping, a small dapper middle-aged man in suit and tie, running along the dark sidewalk past the storefronts and the brick facades, and then across Albany Street and up the courthouse steps.

At the top of the steps the light in the main hallway shone out through the glass doors onto the concrete, but the doors were locked and he stood for a moment in a panic, rattling the doors and pounding on the glass. Finally it occurred to him that it was late Saturday afternoon. So he turned and stumbled back down the steps and immediately began to run again, along the high brick wall of the courthouse toward the corner of the building and then around it and along the sidewalk toward a red light above another door. This door was unlocked and he threw it open and ran down a flight of stairs to the basement. In the first office off the hallway he found Dale Willard, Holt County deputy sheriff, sitting at a desk with his feet up. Willard was clipping his fingernails.

"Where's Bud?" Bird cried. He stood panting at the counter.

Willard looked up at him.

"Where's Bud Sealy?"

"He's not here."

"I can see that. Where is he?"

"Right now? He's at home eating his supper."

"Then Jesus Christ, get him on the phone. Tell him to get over here."

Willard allowed his feet to drop from the desktop and slowly he sat up in the chair. He leaned forward and began to brush the fingernail clippings from his shirtfront onto the green blotter on the desk. He was making a neat pile. "Something bothering you, Ralph?" he said. "You sound a little excited."

"What?" Bird said.

He was still standing behind the office counter, panting and sweating, his face as red as beets and his eyes looking as though they belonged in the head of an alarmed poodle.

"Excited? Listen. By god, if you ain't going to call him, at least reach me that phone so I can. What's his number?"

"No. I imagine I can call him myself," Willard said. "Soon's I know there's a reason to call him. Soon's I have some idea what the hell you're talking about."

"What I'm talking about?" Bird said. But he was shouting now. "I'll tell you what—" Then he seemed to catch himself; he appeared to make an effort to be calm. But it didn't quite work, so that he began to speak now to Willard as though he were addressing an idiot. "What I'm talking about," he said, talking too slowly, "is how that son of a bitch is back in town. That's what I'm talking about. Now call him."

"Sure. But which son of a bitch is that, Ralph?"

"What? You mean you—"

"I mean you haven't said yet."

"Well it's Jack Burdette. Jesus Christ, you've at least heard of him, haven't you? You know who he is, don't you?"

"Yes. I know who Jack Burdette is."

"And you know what he did, don't you?"

"I know what he did. Everyone in Holt County knows what he did."

"Then call Bud Sealy. Goddamn it. Here that—" But again he was shouting. The momentary restraint he had managed to place on himself had disappeared and so he was shouting once more, his face inflamed and outraged above the loosened tie. "Here that son of a bitch is back in town again and he's driving a red Cadillac with California plates. And he's got it parked out in front of the Holt Tavern and if you don't quit asking me these goddamn questions and get up off your fat—"

"That'll do," Willard said. He stood up and leaned toward Bird. "Shut your goddamn mouth."

"—he's going to— What?" Bird said. "What'd you just say?"

"I said, 'Shut your goddamn mouth.' Now go over there and sit down. I'll let you know if I want anything more out of you. In the meantime keep your mouth shut."

Ralph Bird was astonished almost into peace by this. He was not used to being talked to in this way; it made him quiet. He sat down in a chair in the corner and folded his hands like a child. But his eyes were still wild.

Willard stood watching him. Finally he pulled the telephone toward himself across the desk. He dialed the number. While he listened to the phone ring he pushed the wastebasket with his foot until it was beneath the edge of the desk; then with his free hand he swept the neat pile of fingernail clippings into the trash.

When Sealy answered, Willard said. "Bud?"

"Yes."

"Bud. Listen. Ralph Bird is in here and he . . ." Willard went on to tell him what Bird had said.

At his home Sealy listened to Willard talking. When Willard finished telling what he knew, Sealy asked how long ago that was and Willard told him and Sealy said had he checked any of it and Willard said no, he hadn't checked any of it, he wanted to call first, and Sealy said he doubted it but after he'd finished eating he'd drive over to see for himself.

"In the meantime what do you want me to do with Bird?" Willard said.

"What's wrong with him?"

"He's still a little excited."

"Hell," Sealy said. "You figure it out. Take him home to his wife if you can't contain him. At least she can feed him his supper."

"I imagine I can contain him," Willard said.

•

*   *   *

So it was full dark now. The streetlamps shone clearly at the
corners of town, making pale circles of light on the pavement
under the trees. It was that brief anticipatory moment between
six and seven o'clock on a November evening when the shops on
Main Street have all been closed for the weekend, when the
high-school kids haven't yet begun to race up and down Main
Street, when even the Holt Tavern is quiet before the Saturday
night rush and out along the highway there are only three or four
men sitting quietly, drinking at the bar in the American Legion.

At home, after he'd talked to Deputy Willard, Bud Sealy
finished his supper. Then he rose and walked outside into the dark
in front of his house. The stars had come out and, looking at them,
he belched once and felt better. Then he lit a cigarette and got
into the sheriff's car parked in front of his house and drove north
two blocks onto Highway 34, then north again onto Main Street.

Driving up Main Street he passed the water tower and the
bank and the post office and the theater, just as Burdette had done
two or three hours earlier, and soon, a block ahead of him, he
could see the red Cadillac parked at the curb in front of the tavern.
He slowed. When he reached the Cadillac he parked the sheriff's
car behind it so that whoever was driving the Cadillac wouldn't
escape. He released the strap over his gun and got out.

But Burdette didn't appear to have escape or anything else
on his mind. He was still sitting in the front seat. He was slumped
down massively in the seat and his head was thrown back against
the headrest. The light from the corner lamp shone palely onto
his big face and jaw.

Sealy examined him for a moment. Finally he tapped with his
fingers on the roof of the car. Inside the car Burdette opened his
eyes and rolled his head, looking up at Sealy as if the sheriff were
of no interest to him whatsoever.

"Well," Sealy said. "So you come back, did you?"

"That's right," Burdette said. "I come back."

"Hell of a deal."

"That's what I think. I've been sitting here trying to remember what for."

"That so?" Sealy said. "I thought you was smarter than that. I thought you had it all figured out."

"I did once. But I seem to of forgot what a little piss ant place this is. I can't seem to recall now what I wanted here."

"No? Well I imagine we haven't changed so much. Not so you'd notice it anyway. We still get a little upset when somebody does something wrong to us. And afterward decides to disappear."

"That was a long time ago," Burdette said.

"Sure it was. But not long enough, don't you see? And that surprises me. Because I can't imagine what in hell you was thinking of. But I know one thing: you made a mistake coming back here. You never should of did that. Now get out of the car."

Burdette didn't move. "You can't do anything to me," he said. "It's been eight years. The statute's already run out."

"You been talking to lawyers?"

"I talked to a couple of them."

"You wasted your time. That don't mean anything. That don't mean diddly-shit."

"Sure it does. It's the same everywhere."

"No," Sealy said. "It don't mean a thing." He opened the car door. "Now listen to me. I'm through talking. I already been nice."

Burdette refused to move. He sat slumped against the steering wheel of the Cadillac, his head lolled back against the headrest.

"Okay, then," Sealy said. "I told you once. I did do that much." He withdrew the gun from its holster on his belt and suddenly he jammed the short barrel into Burdette's ear.

Burdette sat up. He tried to move his head away. But Sealy followed his head with the gun.

"Jesus Christ," Burdette said. "What in hell you think you're doing?"

"Get out," Sealy said.

Now Burdette did move. He rose up out of the Cadillac and stood onto the pavement, tall, heavy, massive, a presence above the sheriff. He was dressed in plaid shirt and dark pants; he was wearing shoes but no socks. His clothes looked as though he'd been sleeping in them.

"Turn around," Sealy said.

"Now goddamn it, Bud. What the hell?"

Sealy poked him with the gun. "Turn around."

Burdette grunted, but slowly he turned so that his back was toward the sheriff. Sealy removed a pair of handcuffs from his back pocket and locked them around Burdette's thick wrists. It took some effort to get them closed.

"Well Jesus," Burdette said. "You mean to tell me, you mean you're not even going to read me my rights?"

"What rights is that? You don't have no rights. Not no more. Now hold still while I feel you."

"You son of a bitch," Burdette said.

"That's right," Sealy said. "That's just exactly right."

He began to run his hands over Burdette, feeling up and down his pants legs and along the fat over his ribs. He turned his pockets out. When he was satisfied that Burdette was carrying nothing more dangerous than a wallet and some pocket change, he stood for a moment behind Burdette's wide back, staring at the massive and wrinkled shirt.

And yet it was still that quiet hour on Main Street, that brief elusive moment of peace and nothing was moving; there wasn't another person anywhere on the street. And so, without thought, I suppose without even knowing he was going to, while the two of them stood beside the gleaming red Cadillac in that brief tranquillity of a November evening, the sheriff smashed Jack Burdette in the back of the head with the butt of his gun. Burdette howled and fell across the hood of the car. He began to curse.

"No," Bud Sealy said, looking down at the blood trickling from the back of Burdette's head. "I thought you was smarter than that. I did think you knew better than to come back here. What in hell was you thinking of?"

TWO

I had known Jack Burdette all his life. Or all of it, that is, except for the four years in the early 1960s when he was in the Army and in Holt and I was in college and then again later for those eight years after he had disappeared when no one in Holt knew him, that period when he was out in California living on his charm and that sum of money which he must have thought would last him a lifetime until one day the money gave out and he discovered he had only the charm left and not much of that. But yes: I knew him. We had grown up together. For a long time I had even liked him.

His father, whom people here still refer to as John Senior, was a well-known figure in town. He worked at Nexey's Lumberyard on Main Street near the railroad tracks and he was a big man too—like Jack was, or like Jack was to become anyway—with a considerable gut and a big loud voice that was exactly like a bull's bellow and of about that appropriateness. Still he was a likable man, I suppose. People in Holt thought so. He wore pressed overalls to work at the lumberyard, and in the evenings before he went home for supper he always drank for an hour or two in the bars out along Highway 34, in the Legion bar or at the Wagon-wheel Lounge, with some of the other men in town who were his contemporaries.

Jack's mother, on the other hand, was a very small woman, very thin and pinched-looking. She wore scrupulously clean round wire glasses on the bridge of her nose and she combed her hair in a style that would have been fashionable in the 1920s when she was young, a kind of permanent sheared-off bob. She was a very serious woman. She never drank or raised her voice much above a whisper, so we understood in Holt that she tolerated her husband's excesses because she was a good Catholic. She played the organ at St. John's Church and made confession faithfully to old Father O'Brien who wore a hearing aid. She hadn't much else in her life, so it must have been Father O'Brien and the Catholic Church which sustained her.

They lived, during the years I am talking about, over there on the north side of town on Birch Street across the tracks. It was an old yellow stucco house and behind it they had a vacant lot, overgrown with cheat weed and redroot, which ran back for fifty yards toward the fairgrounds. This was the poorer part of town then, before the new tract houses were annexed into the city in the 1970s, but people in Holt still considered the Burdettes to be an average family with adequate income and status. If nothing else, they were interesting. There was sufficient tension in the family to make them worth watching.

Jack was born in 1941. His parents were already in their mid-forties then. They had been married for more than twenty years. So I assume they had long ago stopped expecting ever to have children and had settled into that fractious kind of truce that childless couples often accept in place of real marriage. Then Jack was born. And he was quite unexpected, of course. Consequently his parents tried to patch it up for a while. His father is said to have stopped drinking in the bars for an entire year and people say his mother looked almost pretty for a time, that she appeared to have a kind of glow. But it didn't last. She never became

pregnant again. And soon the old man was drinking regularly in
the bars once more while Jack's mother went back to playing the
organ at the Catholic church on Sunday mornings, where in that
weekly hour of temporary peace she could watch Father O'Brien
from behind those clean little wire glasses of hers. It was all as if
nothing had changed—except that there was a new source of
tension now, and consequently more arguments.

Well, he was a tough kid. He had a shock of black hair and
he was always big for his age. Then when he was six they sent him
to school. With his hair combed flat on his head and dressed in
new shirt and pants, he entered for the first time that old red
three-story brick building on the west edge of town, with its wide
foot-hollowed stairs and its tall windows and that familiar smell
of swept dust, and he didn't like it. At school they expected him
to sit still, to raise his hand and be quiet. So at recess he walked
off the playground and went home. He did this about once a week.
And when he arrived at home Mrs. Burdette, that serious little
pious woman, would take him by the back hair, lean him across
the kitchen table and hit him with the spatula. Then she would
send him back. Except that he didn't always go back; instead he
often wandered about town, through the back alleys behind the
Main Street businesses and out along the railroad tracks into the
country. So in April they decided that another full year of the first
grade and another complete term with Mrs. Peach would do him
good. I don't think they believed that Jack had been fully
socialized yet.

Still I can't imagine that Mrs. Peach had any part in this
decision or that she was excited by it personally. But, in any case,
it was because of that routine first-grade truancy of his that Jack
was there again the next year when I entered school in 1948. And
since his name came after mine in the class rolls he was assigned
the desk behind me. He was already there that first morning. He
had arrived early; his wet-combed hair was stiff on his head and
he was sitting at his desk with his hands folded as if he were bored

with it all already and was merely waiting for a chance to escape. We didn't interest him at all. He was a veteran of the first grade and beyond us. Besides he was at least twenty pounds heavier and a good head taller than we were. We didn't even exist for him yet.

But later, on the second or third day of school—in the middle of the afternoon when it was hot and still in the room and when the old high windows were open to the air and there wasn't any air, and while we were sweating over the alphabet, copying out the letters onto lined sheets of paper—Jack popped me on the head. I turned around. I don't know what I expected. But on his desk there was a dead gopher. He had it stretched out over his attempts at some As and Bs. He had squeezed out a drop of gopher blood onto the paper below his name. "You want him?" he said.

"No," I said. "I don't want him."

"Well I'm done with him."

"I don't want him."

Then Mrs. Peach was standing over us. She was standing back a little too. She ordered Jack to deposit the dead gopher in the trash immediately.

Jack stood up and walked to the front of the room. In the far corner, beside the pencil sharpener where the wastebasket was, he turned and faced us. We were all watching him. He raised the gopher by the hind leg and held it there at eye level for a moment, suspended, as if he were about to make a little magic or as if the gopher itself still knew a trick or two. Then he let it go. It seemed to dive into the wastebasket. When it hit bottom it made a satisfactory bang.

"Jack," Mrs. Peach said. "You sit down."

Jack walked back slowly to his desk. At his desk he faced straight ahead and grinned. So we were not just watching him now. We were staring at him—in wonder and awe, and shocked admiration too.

Meanwhile Mrs. Peach had begun to shout at us: "Children.

•

Children," she shouted. "Get back to work." She began to clap
her hands at us.

But for the rest of the afternoon, at least twice each hour, one
of us would break the lead in his pencil so he could rise and walk
to the front of the room and peer down into the wastebasket and
see the gopher. It was lying on its back with its paws curled
bitterly over its fawn belly. Finally, after enough instances of this,
Mrs. Peach announced that if just one more kid broke the lead
in his pencil we would all stay after school. We were not getting
off to a good start with the alphabet at all, she said.

Thus for eight years he was passed from one grade to the next,
from one old local spinster or balding man to the next one,
passing, being promoted each spring not so much by his own
efforts with books and maps and pencils as by the absolute refusal
of our teachers to have anything more to do with him. (Because
the experiment with Mrs. Peach had failed, of course. Holding
him back hadn't improved on his deportment. And none of the
other teachers would even consider taking him twice.) No, he
wore them all out. In fact when it was their year to have him in
their classrooms our teachers, by the middle of September, were
already counting the days until the end of May. They had big
calendars fastened to the walls with heavy Xs scratched and
double-scratched through the accumulation of finished days, and
one of them, Miss Ermalline Johnson, actually resigned during
Christmas break rather than return for another half year. "I
won't," she told the school board. "I couldn't be responsible if
I did."

Then we entered high school. At Holt County Union High
School—it was redbrick too and three stories high as the grade
school had been, but it stood at the south end of Main Street and
it was more ambitious architecturally; it had square turrets at both
ends and the roof was red tile so that it looked a cross between

a prison and somebody's notion of a Mediterranean palace; you
could see it from a distance, risen up above the stunted elm trees
and hackberries, standing alone at the end of Main as if blocking
passage out of town, the practical and symbolic notion of what
Holt County thought about higher education, standing there for
fifty years and more until in the middle 1960s it was condemned
and they tore it down and sold off the old redbrick for backyard
patios and borders for zinnia beds and replaced it with a new low
one-story pedestrian affair that had a scarcity of windows—it was
there, at Holt County Union High School, that Jack Burdette was
even more of a presence. And I don't mean just in our lives, but
in the life of the entire town.

Because he was bigger now. He was taller and stronger—
taller and stronger than anybody else in school. By the time we
graduated in the spring of 1960 he was six feet four and weighed
two hundred and forty pounds. But he wasn't fat then. He was
still heavily muscled, broad-shouldered and thick-boned. So at
least physically he was more than just that one year ahead of us.
He was like a full grown man among mere children, a colossus
among pigmies. He had already begun to shave the bristle on his
chin in the eighth grade—at a time when the rest of us hadn't
even begun to contemplate peach fuzz yet—and in high school
he had a thick mat of black hair on his chest. It stuck out through
his white tee shirts like little black pins. He was a kind of
high-school boy's high-school boy: the supreme example of what
was possible in the absolute.

The most obvious evidence of this, though—to us and to all
of Holt County—was the fact that he was an excellent athlete.
He started every high-school football game for four years. He
played fullback and linebacker and almost single-handedly made
us worth a damn. The rest of us weren't much good. I wasn't. (I
played end. I was skinny, slow-footed, nearsighted, ignorant of
technique and reluctant to cross the middle; I might manage to
catch a pass if nobody was breathing down my neck, but only if

.

the ball hit me square in the hairless chest.) But Jack was. Jack was something. He was a superb athlete. He was the hotshot that made it all go. When we were juniors he won the northeast conference for us. And when we were seniors he took us to the state championship, through the conference and then the playoffs and finally to the last game—which in the end we managed to lose anyway. We were playing a team from the Western Slope and they had us at a disadvantage: they were able to field more than one real player.

But in high school our teachers had that at least as leverage. Like the rest of us, he was required by state rules to pass at least three-fourths of his classes if he expected to play football. And Jack managed that in his own fashion too. He feigned attentiveness during math and history and English classes—that is, he didn't actually go to sleep—and when he was called on to recite he rose up and made jokes. Then there were shouts of laughter from the boys in the back rows and tittering among the girls up front. In short time our teachers learned not to call on him at all.

Still he had to take tests and turn in papers as we all did. And that's where Wanda Jo Evans came in.

Wanda Jo Evans loved him. I believe, if such a thing is possible, that she even loved him more than he did himself. She adored him, idolized him, worshiped him, hung on him. All of that and no exaggeration either. She wasn't even the only one; she was merely the most obvious and conspicuous about it. Well, she was a nice girl, really pretty and creamy, and still a little plump then too in a high-school-girlish sort of way, a little given to baby fat yet, with strawberry blonde hair and soft gray eyes the color of clouds. She had full breasts too and round white arms. So if she was in love with Jack—and she emphatically was—the rest of us were more than a little in love with her and would gladly have sacrificed that proverbial left appendage of ours to have changed places with him. But Wanda Jo didn't even notice us. She didn't see us. We were mere background and bit-players to her. Or just smoke maybe. For it was Jack alone that she loved.

So of course she helped him. She made neat little precise crib sheets for him and she learned to compose his term papers in his own sprawling and childish hand, receiving as reward for this constant adoration and these daily efforts at school the exclusive right to ride beside him, to hang on his arm in the middle of the front seat of his old Ford pickup while he raced and helled up and down Main Street on Friday and Saturday nights with the gear-shift stuck up between her creamy white knees.

We envied them all of that then. Such things matter in high school. They seem primary at the time, essential. At least they seemed that way to us who were Jack's classmates.

But it was on the football field that he made his real mark during those years. In public, I mean. For, as I have said already, he was a hell of a football player: peerless and incredible and brutal. The whole town thought so. Indeed there are men in Holt today who will still tell you, even taking into account what he did later, that Jack Burdette was the best fullback and linebacker that Holt County ever produced. And no doubt they are right. The coaches from all the area colleges and universities thought so too; they began to pay attention to him when he was still only a sophomore.

Consequently it was about then that his father, old John Senior, began to pay attention to him as well. The old man came to all of the games and when something happened on the field you could hear him yelling obscenely from the stands. Afterward he came down into the locker room and stood around between the benches, smelling of beer and whiskey and slapping us on the shoulder while we got out of our pads. He made drunken little speeches to us. "By god," he'd say. "Goddamn it, you boys, you sure . . ." And so on. His face would be inflamed with the drama of it all, with his own high emotion and the pregame mix of liquor, and then the spit would begin to fly. Meanwhile we would be waiting for him to finish, or at least to get out of the way, so we could take a shower. But he was proud of all the boys, though he was proudest, of course, of Jack. There was a lot to be proud of. In the fall during those years the old man made money by betting on all of the high-school football games with the men from other towns.

Then in the winter of 1959, about a month after we had played our last game, the old man died. That is, he was killed. By a freight train in the middle of town. Later the railroad company would put up crossing guards and flashing lights, but there were neither of these then.

It was early in December on a Saturday night. The old man had been drinking as usual in the Legion. He had been telling stories at the bar in his loud voice and leaning drunkenly on the barmaids whenever they stood beside him to give their orders to the bartender. Pulling the young girls toward himself into his thick arms, he had kissed their cheeks and had asked them his salacious little joke: don't you want to come out to my car and test my heater? When the girls had said no, he had thrown his head back and laughed.

Thus he had had his usual satisfactory time of it, people say. Then the Legion closed. But outside, when they left the bar, they found that it had begun to snow; it was coming down under the streetlights and beginning to collect along the gutters. So the old man drove home in the snow, just as everyone else did that night, except that driving north up Main Street he would have passed the three blocks of stores, shadowy-looking and quiet now, with the store windows decorated for the holiday with cotton and tinsel and the lamp poles at the corners festooned with Christmas lights. And so, feeling pleased with it all, perhaps even feeling a little satisfied with his own place in the great scheme of things, he must have begun to sing. For he was a great singer when he was drunk. Consequently when he came to the railroad tracks at the center of town he didn't hear the train at all or even see it coming. He drove directly onto the tracks and was hit at once.

The next day, on Sunday morning, most of the men in town, and many of the women and children too, came out to look at the car. In the night the snow had stopped and it was very bright and cold.

I was there too, with my father. At the time he was still teaching me to take photographs for the local newspaper, for the *Holt Mercury,* which he owned and edited. When he woke me that morning he said that I should bring the camera.

He parked the car on Main Street and then we got out and walked along the tracks. There were deep scars in the railroad ties where the iron wheels of the old man's Buick had gouged the ties after the rubber had been torn off. The scars made it look as though some madman had plowed a furrow along the railroad tracks with a single-bottom plow. One of the ruined tires was down in the weeds and there was another one ahead of us where we could see the trail it had made in the snow before it tipped over. I took a picture of it.

Then we went on, walking along the tracks beside the train. Ahead of us we could see that there were people gathered around the smashed Buick. It was shoved free of the train now, into the ditch below the engine. There were men and women peering inside the car and talking to one another.

"You had better take photographs of that," my dad said. "But stand up here so you can get the side of the train in it."

I crowded the boxcars and snapped photographs of what I saw through the camera. Then my dad took several pictures too, to be certain he had something suitable for the front page. Afterward he gave the camera back to me and we went on.

When we arrived at the car it was standing upright in the ditch weeds on its bent rims. The driver's door was crushed in, shoved against the passenger's side. In the door there was the deep

·

impact, as in a clay mold or a piece of tin, where the train engine had hit it. All the glass had been popped out and scattered.

Off to the side, George Foley, who was a barber in Holt and who lived near the tracks, was explaining to two or three other men what had happened. My dad and I stopped to hear what he was saying.

He was saying in the night how he had heard a sudden bang and immediately afterward a continuous screeching; he had gotten up to see what it was. The train had almost stopped then, he said, but down the tracks in front of it there was a car that was caught and the car was still being shoved along ahead of the engine and there were sparks flying off into the air. So he had gotten dressed and had run outside down the tracks to the head of the train. By then it was stopped completely. "But it didn't make no difference," he said. "It was already too late. He was already dead."

"How do you know that?" my dad said.

"What?"

"How do you know that he was already dead?"

"Well wouldn't he be?"

"I don't know. I'd like to think he was anyway."

"That's what I mean. If a goddamn freight train hits somebody in the middle of the night and it's going sixty miles a hour—if that don't kill him outright, I don't know what else will."

"Probably," my dad said. "What else did you see?"

"Plenty," George Foley said, "I saw enough."

He told us the men were already out of the train engine by the time he ran up to the car. They were moving about, trying to pull the car away from the front of the engine by hand, but it was stuck fast, enmeshed with the engine, and meanwhile the big headlight still worked back and forth above them, shining down the tracks into the snow. Then he looked inside the car.

"And my god, he was just meat. That's all he was. He was just hamburger with clothes on. And his clothes, why they was just bloody rags."

Then he told us that the police had arrived. However, there was still some confusion about what to do. It would have been faster to have used cutting torches, but there was gasoline dripping out of the car and they were afraid of starting a fire. Finally somebody thought of hydraulic jacks. Just before morning, then, by working in shifts they were able to pry the car loose and to remove the body. They brought it out in pieces. The police took what they could of it over to John Baker at the Holt Mortuary to prepare for burial.

"And I seen it all," Foley told us. "I seen everything."

Then he was finished. There were others walking along the tracks toward us to look at the car: Ed Taylor and Mrs. Taylor, who had come into town to attend church; they were dressed up. Foley walked over to them and began to tell them his story.

My dad watched him for a moment. "That's the trouble with eyewitnesses," he said. "They just think they've seen it all. And every time they tell it they think they have to improve on what they've already told somebody else."

"Didn't you believe any of it?" I said.

"Maybe. But George Foley likes to hear himself talk. It's how he makes his living."

"I thought he was a barber."

"He is."

"Oh," I said.

"So now I'm going over to the depot," my dad said, "to see if I can find the engineers. I want to hear what they have to say. Then I'll check with the police. In the meantime you can take some more pictures."

He walked away toward the depot. I didn't know what more he had in mind for me to take pictures of. But I moved around to the far side of the car and took several photographs from that angle, with the car in the foreground and the train risen up black and massive behind it. There was still snow on the ground where people had tracked it and the contrast of the snow and the train should have made a good picture, but I forgot about facing into the sun so that later when the photographs were developed it all looked washed out. There was a lot that I didn't know yet.

When I had finished I decided I wanted to look inside the car. I hadn't done that yet and thought I wanted to. Afterward I was sorry I had. There was blood on the crushed dashboard and there were ragged bits of the old man's coat stuck to the driver's door. And hanging from one of the rags was a flap of skin which still had hair growing from it. I felt sick. I walked away from the car back along the tracks toward Main Street.

I intended to wait for my dad in our car, where we had parked it at the curb in front of Kinsey's Hardware. But before I got there I met Jack Burdette.

Jack was alone. He was walking toward me along the tracks in his winter coat; his face looked pasty and he hadn't shaved yet. I stopped when we were close to one another.

"Did you see it?" he said.

"Yes. But I'm sorry about your father."

"Everybody is," he said.

Then I didn't know what to say. I thought of warning him. But I didn't.

He went on and I turned to watch him walk along the tracks. Beside the train he looked cold and dark and solitary. Then he reached the car and I could see that George Foley had discovered him. Foley was already beginning to talk. He put his arm around Jack, while the other people stepped back a little, but I didn't want to watch it. I knew what Foley had to tell him. I went on and got into our car and turned the heater on and waited for my dad to come back from the depot.

THREE

They buried Jack's father on the following Tuesday in the Holt County Cemetery northeast of town. In the nights preceding the funeral there was a wake, then on the day of the funeral there was a Mass of the Dead in the morning at St. John's Church. Afterward, outside, it was very cold standing at the gravesite. Old Father O'Brien said quickly what he had to over the closed casket and spoke in Latin while he scattered ashes. When it was over those of us who attended the gravesite rites filed past Jack and his mother and took off our gloves to shake their hands. Then we went home, or back to school or back to work, and they were left alone.

Things were tight then. Don Nexey, who owned the lumberyard, gave Mrs. Burdette a check equal to two months of her husband's salary—which was generous of him, people said; he wasn't required to do that—but the extra money would not have gone far, probably not much beyond the cost of the funeral and the old man's casket. As a result, in the middle of January Mrs. Burdette, who had never worked outside the home before, took a job at Duckwall's Store on Main Street. They hired her as a clerk. And every day now if you looked through the big display windows you could see her inside the store, wearing a thin green smock

over her plain dresses and standing at the cash register or working
farther back, dusting and tidying the racks of picture frames and
cheap toys. In this way they still had a small regular income each
month and I suppose by being very frugal were able to make ends
meet. Still I don't think money was the only consideration. At
school we began to notice that Jack had changed. He was brooding
and surly now. Things had gotten difficult for him.

It had to do with his mother. I think Mrs. Burdette believed
that she had been given a new chance. It was as if she thought with
the old man's death that she had been given a fresh opportunity.
To save Jack, I mean; to prevent his becoming what she had only
been able to tolerate in his father—tolerate simply because, given
her beliefs and the tenor of the times, the thought of divorce was
completely and utterly *in*tolerable. So she tried to assert herself.
I suppose she even harbored the notion that Jack might yet turn
out to be one of God's children and suffered to come unto Jesus.
I don't know. I can't say what went on in her head or how she
thought. But I know that Jack was pretty miserable for a time. And
I don't think it had a lot to do with grieving over his father's death.

This went on for about two months, until about the end of
February. Then he broke with her. He did something which
alienated his mother forever and which at least temporarily
astonished the rest of us. And looking at it now in retrospect, it
seems to have established a pattern for him—or to have con-
firmed one anyway—a pattern which involved both a sudden
move and a rash concomitant act. He left his mother and moved
into the Letitia Hotel.

It was an old ramshackle two-story frame building with a deep
long porch on its north side. It was built in 1914 by an early
resident, an Irishman who had arrived some twenty years earlier
as a small boy in the company of his parents. Then the mother

died of influenza while he, the immigrant boy, watched, and so years later when he built the hotel he gave it her name out of lingering grief and old affection. It stood (and still stands, though a rooming house now for old men and migrant laborers and drunks) on the corner of Second and Ash streets, a block west of Main. Across the street there is an old hackberry tree which isn't doing very well. The local historical society claims that it was one of the first trees planted in Holt County and they've erected a cement curb around it to protect it.

Jack's room was on the second floor. There wasn't much in it: an old iron bed and wooden dresser and a gauzy-curtained window overlooking Second Street. It didn't have any sink or bathroom; the only bathroom on the second floor was at the end of the hall, a space about the size of a walk-in closet. But it didn't cost much to room at the hotel and he took his meals (when he wasn't eating at Wanda Jo Evans's house or with one of the rest of us) in the little dining room on the first floor.

He paid for these—the rent and the occasional dinners—by working at the Farmers' Co-op Elevator beside the railroad tracks. He had first begun to work at the elevator in the summer when he was sixteen. They had put him to work scooping wheat and unloading grain trucks and running the big augers. Now he began to work there in the afternoons after school and on the weekends as well. The work suited him exactly. It gave him another opportunity to sweat, to display that considerable strength of his, to expand himself amongst the exhaust of trucks and the clouds of grain dust. They were even paying him something for his efforts. Then, too, there was always that rough backslapping of the men who worked there, their sardonic talk and their jokes. For the men liked him, of course: Jack was a local phenomenon. They talked football to him. They remembered each game he had played better than he did himself, and not just the scores but the individual plays and the records he had set as well. They kidded

him, they slapped his back; it was a kind of grown-man's adu-
lation, a form of praise he needed and enjoyed.

So now, once he had left his mother's house, he had all of that
again, every day. But also, for the first time, he had a room he
could call just his and the liberty to come and go from it as he
would, with a steady diet of free meals, or at least cheap ones, and
enough money left over in his pocket to spend on beer and poker
and nickel cigars, and still enough left over to buy gas to put in
his pickup and then occasionally even something yet remaining
to spend on Wanda Jo Evans. Because he wasn't cheap: if Jack had
money he always spent it. So he might take her out to a movie,
say, or treat her to a hamburger at the Holt Cafe, with an order
of French fries on the table between them to share equally. Then
we would see them together: Wanda Jo leaning toward him across
the table, her hand with the gripped hamburger arrested before
her face, while he talked and ate and chewed and while she went
on watching him out of those gray and wondering eyes.

But what I remember most about that time were those
evenings in the hotel room. Jack and the rest of us would be
playing poker. We would be betting our nickels and dimes at a
wooden box upended in the center of the room, under that high
old ceiling, under that single dim light bulb suspended from a
cord, while off in the corner sitting on the bed Wanda Jo Evans
would be bent over the books and the cheap tablets on her lap.
She would be attempting to complete Jack's and her own English
and math assignments in time to hand them in the next morning,
and only now and then would she even stop long enough to look
up from under her strawberry hair, to glance quickly at Jack when
he laughed or thought to say something that included her.

We played most of these poker games on Sunday nights.
There would be beer then too. Jack was nineteen and the rest of
us were eighteen now. We were legally of an age not only to be
drafted to fight this country's wars but to buy beer too, which if
we drank enough of it, and God knows we tried, would give us

the necessary recklessness and the urge to shout that we believed were essential for any poker game involving high-school boys.

We had a good time that winter and spring. At school it became a point of honor and a matter of high privilege to say that you had been allowed to sit in, that you had entered Jack's room at the hotel and had lost your dollar or two at cards on Sunday night and had drunk a six-pack of beer. It gave you the right to boast the next morning—on Monday, at Holt County Union High School—to boast and complain of a headache while old Mrs. Lindquist tried once more to explain to us *The Importance of Being Earnest*.

But there was at least one snag in these Sunday night proceedings: the beer was warm. It had to be bought on Saturday night because none of the bars or liquor stores was open in Holt on Sunday. And since Jack's room didn't have an ice chest or a refrigerator (and since none of the rest of us was quite fool enough to store the beer at home in his own refrigerator where his mother would sure as hell find it and ask questions), the beer, by Sunday night, was approximately the temperature of blood.

We attempted several solutions to this problem. We tried, for example, stacking the cartons of beer on the window ledge outside Jack's room. And that kept it cool overnight, but sometimes it kept it too cool: it froze. Then we had Popsicles while we played cards. Which was a funny thing for a while. But the bite was gone out of the beer. It was like kissing your own sister, Bobby Williams said.

"Hell," Jack said. "It's more like kissing my old lady. Which ain't even worth trying once."

In the middle of that next week, then, after midnight, Jack Burdette and Tom Crossland and Bobby Williams and I crowded into the cab of Jack's old pickup. Wanda Jo Evans was there too. Jack was driving and Wanda Jo was sitting on my lap—which was about as close to a high-school boy's notion of heaven as I was ever to come. We drove across town that way. Then Jack eased the

pickup into the alley behind Burcham Scott's old house. When
we entered the alley Jack turned the lights off and coasted to a
stop. Then we got out and whispered to one another and slunk
along in the dark away from the pickup into the old man's
backyard, past his cement-block incinerator and his fallow garden
and finally up onto his back porch, where, pushed off into a
corner, there was an ancient Majestic refrigerator which everyone
in Holt County knew about. It was a part of the legend we'd all
grown up with. We all knew that Burcham Scott was a fisherman,
that he was an old freckled-headed man who had long ago retired
from the pretense of ever doing anything else but fish and we
knew the refrigerator was a part of his equipment. He kept his
night crawlers and red worms in the refrigerator so they would
stay lively and unspoiled until he needed them.

But it was only the middle of March now, too early for
Burcham to begin fishing again, so the refrigerator was empty and
unplugged. We began to slide it away from the wall. Then we tried
to pick it up. But we were fumbling in the dark and the porch
was narrow and we kept bumping into one another. Finally Jack
hissed:

"Get back, you damn morphadites. I'll do it myself."

And he did. He was that big, that strong. He stooped in front
of it, threw his arms around the old Majestic as if it were no more
than some heavy tractable farm girl who had come into town for
a squeeze and a dance, and then stood up with it. He turned,
pivoting, and waltzed off the porch with the refrigerator hugged
up into his arms and carried it out to the alley, while behind him
Bobby Williams and Tom Crossland and I followed like children,
punching one another and giggling.

At the pickup Jack said: "You think one of you runts could
at least open the goddamn tailgate?"

So we drove back across town that night with the old
refrigerator riding up white and square in the back of the pickup,
the four of us sitting around it while Wanda Jo Evans drove, and

at the hotel we didn't even attempt to help him. We merely held the hotel door open while he lifted the refrigerator out of the pickup once more and then carried it against his chest, as if it were still only a farm girl or a crate of peaches, say, on up the stairs to his room. There we opened that door for him too and watched him set it down.

He was panting a little now. There was a thin sheen of sweat on his face. While he caught his breath Wanda Jo plugged it in. Then Jack produced a six-pack of beer. He centered the beer ceremoniously on a shelf in the refrigerator, shut the door, looked around at us, then opened the door again. "There," he said. "Now don't that scratch your ass? Which one of you boys wants a cold beer?"

"Jesus Christ," I said. "It's all the comforts of home, Jack."

"You goddamn right it is."

"And there ain't no place like home," Bobby said.

"No, there ain't," Tom Crossland said. "Oh Dorothy, come and fuck me."

"What in hell's that supposed to mean?"

"Home," he said. "The *Wizard of Oz*."

"Well watch your goddamn language," Jack said. "There's a woman present."

We all looked at Wanda Jo. Wanda Jo looked lovely. She was smiling at Jack as if what he had said was not only chivalrous but clever.

And that set us off. Snorting and laughing, we pounded Jack on the back and shared the six-pack of beer out among ourselves. And though the beer wasn't cold yet, it didn't matter. It was cold in theory. So we began to tell and retell the story, inventing new twists in the string of events and speculating frequently upon the look on Burcham Scott's old face the next morning when he would walk out onto his back porch. He'd scratch himself and look flat dumbfounded, we said. He'd misplace his worm, Bobby Williams said.

About two o'clock we finished the beer. We left Jack at the
hotel with Wanda Jo and went home. The other boys lived out
in the country, but I lived in town on Cedar Street.

When I arrived at the house that night and mounted the stairs
I found that my father was waiting up for me. That is, he was in
bed but he was still awake. "Pat," he said.

"Yes sir?"

"Come here."

I stopped in the doorway. He was lying in bed beside my
mother. She was asleep but my dad had been reading. His glasses
were pushed up onto his forehead and the reading lamp shone
down onto his face. His face looked very white.

"Son," he said. "I've just been wondering."

"About what?"

"Son, you ever figure on making anything of yourself?"

"I hope to."

"Do you?" he said. "That's a comfort. But I'm just curious:
when do you plan on starting?"

But Jack Burdette didn't have a father anymore to wait up for
him, to question him about his intentions—not that old John
Senior would ever have done much of that anyway, even if he were
still alive—but now the old man wasn't available even to pretend
that he might; and of course Jack had already broken with his
mother. So, for him, this episode with Burcham Scott's Majestic
refrigerator became just one more piece in the growing legend.
It became just one more feature in that local aura that was already
following him around high school and about the town. For we had
all begun to expect the unusual of him by that time, while he, for
his part, had already learned—if acting on bent and sheer heedless
volition can be said to be a form of learning—not to disappoint
the expectations of anyone. Least of all his own.

Thus he finished his senior year at Holt County Union High School in style. He lived upstairs in the Letitia Hotel. He worked every day at the Co-op Elevator among grown men who admired him. He played poker with his friends in a room he had paid for himself. And on Sunday nights he drank cold beer that had been chilled in somebody else's refrigerator. It was a high-school boy's dream of a dream.

Except that there turned out to be one final hitch in this too: while most of the adults in town and even the high-school principal took a tolerant view of Jack's activities, Arnold Beckham did not. Arnold Beckham was the sheriff. He was one in the long string of Bud Sealy's elected predecessors and he wasn't stupid. He understood that this weekly teenage hell-raising might not only endanger his reelection the next time he ran for sheriff but that it might even reduce the amount of his eventual hard-earned pension. He couldn't tolerate that. Consequently he took measures to protect himself.

One night about midnight, toward the end of April, Sheriff Beckham climbed up the narrow stairs at the hotel and knocked on the door to Jack's room. It was a Sunday night and as usual four or five of us were playing cards When we heard the knock there was sudden quiet in the room. Jack nodded at Wanda Jo Evans, who rose obediently from the bed in the corner. She had been doing Jack's homework. Now, still carrying a textbook and one of the cheap tablets under her arm, she crossed to the door and opened it slightly.

"Wanda Jo," Arnold said. "You tell that boyfriend of yours to come out here."

Wanda Jo shut the door.

"Now what?" one of us whispered. "Jesus, he's going to tell my folks."

"Stop your crying," Jack said. "I'll handle this."

He stood up from the wooden box in the center of the room

and stepped out into the hallway. We could see Arnold through the open door.

"Sheriff," Jack said. "What can I do for you?"

Arnold Beckham was a short man with a wiry ring of black hair above his ears. He looked Jack up and down. Then he began to speak. It was as if, on his way over, he had prepared a speech.

"Now look," he said. "I know what's going on in there and I know who's in there with you. And I don't care a damn what you do or who you do it with. But by god, boy, the first time somebody calls me up in the middle of the night complaining how his kid ain't home in bed yet, or somebody else says there's empty beer bottles scattered all over their petunia patch—well by god, boy, I'll close you down so fast you won't have time to kiss it good-bye or even hide your beer. You understand me?"

"On what charge?" Jack said.

"You ain't listening," Arnold Beckham said. Then he did something none of us expected. He reached up and grabbed Jack's shirt at the throat and pulled Jack's big face down toward his own. "I don't need no charge," he said. "On whatever comes to mind."

"Let go. We'll keep it quiet. You don't have to worry."

"No, now," Arnold said. He twisted the shirt tighter in his fist. "You still ain't listening. Because I'm not going to worry. See? I'm not the one that's going to worry."

"All right. We'll keep it down. Now let go. You're messing my shirt up."

"Am I? Well tough titty."

Then Sheriff Beckham stared into Jack's eyes. Their faces were only inches apart. But finally he released him.

"So is that all you wanted?" Jack said.

"No, that is not all I wanted," Arnold Beckham said. "I'd like a fishing cabin in the mountains and a young girl waiting on me. And just now I wisht I was in bed. But that'll do for starters. Now you mind what I said."

He turned then and we could hear him walking back down

the narrow hallway. But he stopped before he reached the stairs. "And you tell that little girl of yours to go home now. I seen her mom leaving the hospital already." Then he went on.

Jack reentered the room and closed the door. He sat down at the wooden box again. We were all watching him, looking for proof that something had registered. But it hadn't. All Jack said was: "Wanda Jo. You heard what Arnold said. Your old lady's got off her shift at the hospital. So you better leave that homework till tomorrow." Then he smoothed his shirt over his chest once more. And gathering up his cards, he said: "Now who dealt this goddamn mess?"

So the point of all that was wasted on Jack. He had had his first brief taste of law and authority. He had been warned officially. But the warning hadn't meant much to him. It had merely meant that he had to be more careful, a little more circumspect. It never occurred to him that he might have to alter in any real way whatever he wanted to do. I suppose to him it was like a complicated play in football—a double reverse, say, with a fake dive into the middle, by which you could still score, only it would take a little more practice and finesse to do it. It was merely a lesson in subtlety, a brief instruction in the need for secrecy.

And so at the end of May he graduated from high school. We all did: Wanda Jo Evans and Bobby Williams and Tom Crossland and the rest of us.

Jack was almost comical in his cap and gown. The red mortarboard was perched like a pinwheel at the back of his head and the crimson gown he wore was at least three sizes too small for him; it was stretched tight across his shoulders and the hem of it stopped at his knees. He looked a joke, a travesty, like some form of Paul Bunyan who had been gotten up for a kindergartener's promotion or a pigmies' ball. But when his name was called he rose dutifully, even proudly, from his seat in the auditorium.

Then he stomped up across the stage in his cowboy boots and accepted the diploma from the president of the school board as if the diploma were something he actually valued.

In the evening we got drunk with one another for the last time. Afterward we went our separate ways. Bobby Williams and Tom Crossland went to work for their fathers, farming. Wanda Jo Evans stayed in Holt, where she was employed at the phone company as a secretary. And Jack and I went off to college, to study at the university in Boulder. I had in mind to study journalism, in the attempt to begin making something of myself as my father had suggested. And what Jack had in mind was to play football. He had an athletic scholarship, a full ride. The coaches at the university were willing to ignore the Ds on his transcript if he was willing to get his nose dirty. And of course he was.

So we had that in common that summer after graduation: we were both going to college at Boulder. It served as another bond between us. Whenever we met during the summer we talked about college and explained to one another just what kind of splash we intended to make. When we got there, though, it didn't turn out quite the way we intended: one of us sank and the other barely made a ripple. Boulder was a deeper pond than a couple of boys from Holt County had anticipated.

FOUR

But it was all right in the beginning. He was a big rawboned kid and when he showed up for football practice in the middle of August he was sufficiently violent to please the coaches. Still it must have been obvious that he wasn't a college-level running back. He was big but he was too slow. So in the second or third week of practice the coaches moved him into the line. That way he could use his strength and aggressiveness and not have to think too much. But he missed the glory. In high school he had carried the ball himself and had had his name featured prominently in the local papers. Now he was a defensive tackle and while he was still pretty good, everyone in college was good; so he wasn't singled out for special attention.

Then school started. I had arrived by that time myself. I had moved into the dorm with another freshman, a scrawny red-haired kid from Chicago named Stewart Fliegelman. I had never met anyone like Fliegelman before. As soon as I'd unpacked my bags he announced that he had come out West as a missionary, to spread the gospel according to Marx. He was full of that kind of youthful enthusiasm. But I enjoyed him a great deal, and the truth is I still miss him. He's a lawyer now in Oak Park, working

on a second marriage with two sets of kids to provide for, but
about twice a year I call him up and we talk on the phone.

As a roommate Fliegelman was lively, opinionated, verbal,
well-read, studious, disorganized, bighearted and politically rad-
ical. He used to say that my beliefs were quaint, that whatever
charm I had was the direct result of my universal ignorance.
Whenever he said such things I told him to go to hell. I told him
that coming from Chicago he wouldn't know the difference
between bullshit and chocolate pie even if he stepped in it. Then
he would jump me and we'd wrestle in the room. By the end of
that first semester we were close friends and during the four years
that I knew him in Boulder I learned as much from him as I did
from anyone else in the world. I'd never tell him that, though.
He'd say that I was getting sloppy again. He'd say: "Arbuckle, for
once in your life try not to confuse opinion with facts. You're
supposed to be a journalist, for Chrissakes."

And so I am. Or at least I try to be. And the IRS, for their
part, think so too: they continue to accept my claim to be a
newspaperman without ever demanding to see the actual prod-
uct. Besides, I keep a framed diploma hanging on the wall above
my desk to further substantiate my claim. The diploma's been
there for more than twenty years. It's dust-coated and spider-
webbed now and the paint behind it is darker than the rest.
Because, in the end, after four years of college, I came home again.
It was my father's idea; he wanted me to help run the paper and
eventually to take it over. At the time it sounded like a good thing
to do. And so I've been here ever since, for twenty years and more,
trying once a week to get out a small-town newspaper for the
edification and entertainment of the local populace, if not for the
profit and remuneration of its editor and publisher: the *Holt
Mercury*.

But that was later. In the fall of 1960 I was in college. And
so was Jack Burdette. For a while yet.

After I'd arrived in Boulder and moved into the dorm I'd still see him occasionally. He'd be on campus with some of the others, big muscular kids wearing athletic tee shirts, filling up the sidewalk coming toward you or occupying a table with some of those good-looking long-legged sorority girls, all of them loud and joking, in the University Memorial Center. But I didn't see him very often and we didn't have much to do with one another then.

He was living in Baker, one of the other dormitories. It was like all of the buildings at the university, constructed of flagstone and brick and red tile. For it was a pretty campus, one of the most beautiful in all of this Rocky Mountain region, with the abrupt sides of the Flatirons standing up at the start of the mountains just above town, and on the campus itself the big trees and the old evergreens and all the red-tiled buildings, with still sufficient space between them so that you didn't feel stifled or closed in by the mass of stone or the press of trees. It was a good place for someone like me to be. Boulder—and living with Fliegelman— opened my eyes.

But none of that was true for Jack. He wasn't there long enough. Not that he would have allowed his vision to have been changed appreciably even if he had been. But he didn't get the chance. Within a month after school started he got into trouble. The trouble had to do with a radio.

I first heard about it—or knew about it, that is—when I saw the article in the *Colorado Daily*. They ran it in a little box on the second page. The article said that another freshman named Curtis Harris had brought charges against Jack and that the student judiciary would convene on Friday to hear the case. The article appeared on Tuesday morning. After reading it I went over to Baker to see if I could find Jack in his dorm room. His roommate, another football player, said he didn't know where Jack was; he was probably watching TV.

"But doesn't he have classes?" I said. "It's the middle of the morning."

"What classes?" he said. "Jack doesn't go to classes."

"You mean today?"

"I mean any day. He hasn't been to a class in three weeks. He's going to get in trouble."

"He's already in trouble," I said.

The guy studied me for a moment. "What's that to you? You know him, or something?"

"I know him," I said. "And they should have given Wanda Jo Evans a scholarship too if they expected Jack to go to class."

"Who's she?"

"You wouldn't know her."

"I know some girls."

"But you wouldn't know her. Anyway where's this TV Jack might be watching?"

"Downstairs. Only I don't know if he's even there. I'm not his keeper."

"I'll go see if I can find him," I said.

I went back downstairs.

After looking around for a few minutes I found Jack in one of the rooms next to the dormitory lounge. The door was shut. He was the only person in the room and he was lying on a sofa in his blue jeans and gray tee shirt. He was watching a game show on the black-and-white television and his feet were sticking out over the end of the sofa. When I sat down near him he looked over at me and then turned back to the TV.

"Jack," I said. "How's it going?"

"I can't complain."

"That's good," I said. "But what do you think will happen?"

"About what?"

"About this radio you took."

"How'd you hear about that? You been talking to somebody?"

"It was in the student paper this morning. I came over to see what you're going to do about it."

"What the hell is there to do about it?"

"Well. The paper said somebody named Curtis Harris filed charges against you. That you stole his radio."

"That's a lie. Hell, he wasn't using it so I just borrowed it for a while. And then I didn't give it back to him yet."

"Are you going to?"

"Not now."

"How come?"

"Because. I don't have it no more. The police have it. They took it for evidence."

"All right, then. But what do you think's going to happen?"

"I already told you: I don't know. Besides, what difference does it make?"

"They might kick you out of school. That's one thing."

"I'm sick of school."

"How do you know that? I mean, Jesus, you haven't even been to classes yet."

"I've been to enough. It's just talk."

I continued to look at him. There were dark bruises on his arms from practicing football and there was a scab on his nose between his eyes. Looking at him, he seemed exactly like a kid who'd fallen off a bicycle, like a great big kid who was now consoling himself by watching television from the living room couch.

"But listen," I said. "Think about it for a minute. Isn't there something we can do about this?"

He stopped watching TV, briefly. He looked at me. "Yeah," he said. "You can loan me some money. I missed breakfast. You can do something about that if you want to."

So I did. I gave him a couple of dollars. I was glad to do that much for him and was ready to do more, although I couldn't have said then what it might have been. He folded the bills I gave him and put them away in his jeans pocket. I watched him for a while longer. But when he didn't say anything more I left. He was still lying on the couch watching somebody else win money in a California studio. That seemed to please him.

Then on Friday, when his hearing came up, the student judiciary found against him. It was an open-and-shut case and after they had heard the evidence they recommended that he be expelled from school. There had been a number of thefts on campus already that fall. Consequently the administration accepted the students' recommendation and decided to make an example of him. But it didn't matter to Jack what they did; he didn't contest the charges or even defend himself. In fact he didn't even attend the hearings. Instead that morning he had gone to the Army recruiter on campus and had enlisted; so now he was obligated to two years of military service, and the Army was glad to have him swell their numbers.

He came over to see me before he went back to Holt. He said he didn't have to report to boot camp until the end of October and he thought he'd go home in the meantime and work at the elevator and see Wanda Jo Evans. He wasn't dissatisfied by the turn of events at all.

"Well," I said. "Maybe it's for the best."

"Why not?" he said. "I might even learn something in the Army."

"Take care, then."

"But just a minute. You got any more money?"

"Probably."

"Because I could use something to get home on."

So Jack Burdette went back to Holt County where he was still a hero and where no one knew about Curtis Harris's radio, or would have cared very much if they had known about it; and then at the end of October he went off to Texas, to boot camp at Fort Bliss. I doubt that the irony of that name occurred to him since he wasn't one to pay much attention to such things and I don't suppose the Army is either. Anyway he was there for almost two months. Then I saw him again just after boot camp was finished. Before being reassigned he had come home on leave and I had gone home at semester break. It was Christmastime. Jack looked thinner and harder now, although it might have been just that his head had been shaved; his cropped head made his neck look taller and now his ears stuck out. In any case all the time he was home he insisted on wearing his uniform and his Army cap about the town. He stayed at the Letitia Hotel while he was home, sleeping through most of the day in his room and spending his nights at the tavern with Wanda Jo Evans, the two of them drinking late into the night while Jack told her stories about things he'd already seen and done in basic training in Texas. I don't know how she stayed awake for all of that since she still had to get up early in the morning to work as a secretary at the phone company every day. But she did; she stayed awake; and it was obvious that if anything she was even more in love with him than she had been before. Then he left again, for Fort Ord in California where he underwent two more months of training—as an assistant machine gunner this time—and afterward he was sent overseas to Germany. So none of us saw him again until he was finally discharged late in 1962. He had stories about all of it. He had liked the Army.

In the meantime I was still in college. By the end of my sophomore year I had managed to pass most of the required courses that everyone had to take and so I was beginning to concentrate on journalism. Much of the classwork was mere theoretical posturing, of little practical use once I had returned to Holt two years later to work on the *Mercury* where people were more interested in who had visited whom over the weekend than they were in the ethical paradoxes presented in the First Amendment. But I didn't know that yet. So I attended class regularly and

took notes, and when I was a junior I began to cover various
campus events for the *Colorado Daily*. It was heady stuff for a while.
It was just beginning to be a willful and exciting time on campus
and at the paper we had the illusion that we were a part of it all
and that we were speaking in the voice of the people even if the
people didn't know it yet or want us to. I remember, for example,
that it was about this time that Barry Goldwater came to speak
on campus and in the paper we said that Goldwater was a fascist,
no better than a murderer. After this statement appeared there
was a considerable outcry all over the state and finally the
chancellor was compelled to remove the student editor who was
responsible for it. Then there were demonstrations on campus.
The due processes of law had been abrogated and we all felt hot
about it. But the editor was never reinstated and it turned out to
be a lost cause.

Still I was beginning to get hot about something else just then.
I had met Nora Kramer by that time and for a year or more she
seemed very much like a lost cause too.

NOW I am not very eager to talk about Nora Kramer. And
certainly she is less than eager to have me talk about her. For Nora
was—and is—a very private person and she will no doubt resent
this invasion of her privacy. But I can't help that: like it or not
she is a part of this account. We were together for eighteen years,
after all, and we had a daughter together. And it was only a good
deal later, after Nora left Holt and and moved to Denver, that I
turned finally, out of loneliness and admiration and love too,
toward Jessie Burdette, who was as different from Nora Kramer
as fire is from ice.

But my god, she was a beautiful young woman when I first
knew her in Boulder. She had astonishing black hair then. It was
as dark and shiny as coal and wonderfully thick and clean. And
her skin was so white that it was like porcelain, or like ivory, and

it was almost transparent so that you felt that if you were only permitted to look at her long enough you might actually see the slow movement of blood at her temples and wrists. She was a very small person, very bright and intelligent and all neat and tidy, and she seemed as self-sufficient as a bird.

But she was living with her father at the time. Dr. Kramer was a well-known professor on campus. He wore bow ties and dark suits to class every day and taught graduate seminars in the English Department. His concentration was in the Puritans. He was great for John Bunyan and thought *The Pilgrim's Progress* was literature. He had studied at Yale as an undergraduate and I believe he considered the students at Colorado to be beneath his abilities. Nevertheless he had been able to resign himself to teaching at Colorado for more than thirty years. He was not a lot of fun to meet in the living room when I called on Nora for a date.

I never knew her mother. Mrs. Kramer had died a number of years earlier. I have seen pictures of Mrs. Kramer, though. The pictures show her to have been a small woman with dark hair like her daughter's, parted severely to one side, and she appears to have had a thin little mouth, which at least while she was being photographed she held tightly closed. But I know very little about her; Nora did not talk readily about her mother. For Mrs. Kramer had died horribly when Nora was eleven years old. And Nora had seen it happen.

She told me about it once, just once, speaking in a monotone voice as if she were reporting some event which had happened not to her but to someone else, as if what had occurred when she was eleven didn't concern her at all anymore.

It happened that she and her mother had gone to Denver on a Saturday morning to shop at May D & F's, which was a big department store downtown, and it was just before Christmas, a bright clear day, so the sidewalks were crowded with people carrying packages and calling pleasantly to one another, dropping coins into the red Salvation Army buckets. And then while she

and her mother were standing at the street corner waiting for the
light to change, Mrs. Kramer had been pushed or jostled by the
crowds so that she was shoved off the curb out into the path of
one of the big city buses that was coming up the street. Mrs.
Kramer was able to avoid being hit head-on by the bus, but as it
went by, her winter coat was caught by something and suddenly
she was being pulled along beside it; then she lost her footing and
she was being dragged along on her back beneath the bus. Nora
began to run after her. But the bus driver didn't see her, or see
her mother either, apparently. Then up the block Nora saw that
her mother's coat had torn free, so that she was no longer being
pulled along the street on her back. But though her mother had
stopped moving, the bus hadn't. And then Nora saw the black
wheels of the bus roll over her mother's chest and head. She
stopped running then. She began to scream. She screamed and
screamed, she told me, until finally someone came and put his coat
over the thing in the street, which had been her mother, and she
remembers that she continued to scream until the ambulance
arrived at last and one of the attendants gave her a shot. Later at
the hospital she was asked to provide identification. She was able
to do that. But when she was asked whom they should call, she
couldn't remember her father's phone number and she began to
scream once more.

   She told me this story one night in our bedroom, early in our
marriage. Afterward I turned in the bed and held her and brushed
my hand over her face, expecting tears on her cheeks. But there
weren't any tears. And after a while she went to sleep. Then the
next morning she would not say anything more about it.

   Thus, so far as I know, that long-ago Saturday morning in
Denver was the last time that Nora Kramer ever screamed about
anything. She would not allow herself to show intense emotion
ever again. Not even when Toni, our daughter, was sixteen and
there was good reason to show emotion.

   But no: I do not wish to cause her further harm. She's had

enough. I am not at all eager to stir up things for her. I am merely glad she seems to be happy again. Still I do feel compelled to make this account of things as accurate as I can. For my own reasons.

But perhaps it's enough to say that after two years of dating Nora Kramer in Boulder, after two years of turning myself inside out for her, so that I hardly knew myself who I was anymore, and after meeting her father repeatedly in the living room where he would be sitting in a chair beside a lamp, reading Bunyan and maybe a little of Milton too, a little of *Paradise Lost* for variety's sake, to clear his palate—those nights when I tried to make conversation with him while he read and while I waited for his black-haired daughter to come down the stairs so we could leave the house and go outside where I thought I might remember how to breathe once more—after all of that Nora and I were married in the summer of 1964 and we moved to Holt where I began to work for my father on the local paper. But Nora didn't like Holt very much, even from the beginning. It wasn't a thing like Boulder and Denver were. And I recall now what Stewart Fliegelman said about our prospects.

"What's wrong with you?" he said. "You still think she's some kind of violin and you just haven't learned the fingering yet?"

"What'd you say?"

"I said, 'She isn't a violin,' for Chrissakes. Aren't you listening to me?"

"I'm trying to," I said. "But it's so goddamn loud in here I can't hear anything. And you never make any sense anyway."

Then Fliegelman leaned across the picnic table and started to shout into my face.

We were sitting in the Sink, one of the student bars on the hill near campus. You sat on wood benches at picnic tables; the tables were all carved and scarred on top and around you all of the walls and the low ceiling were painted black. There were beatnik sayings and slogans on the walls, spray-painted over the black in dripping colors, and toward the back there was a room which had a dirt floor. It was always crowded in the Sink, but it was especially crowded on Friday nights when everyone was trying to make a date for the weekend: an intense place then, packed and smoky and loud and really filthy and still wonderful, with students drunk on the seventy-five-cent pitchers of beer and shouting to people three feet in front of them above the scream of the jukebox. It was the place to go on a Friday night if you were a student in Boulder. It and Tulagi's. Tulagi's had a big dance area and live music while the Sink had atmosphere and also Sink Burgers with special sauce that ran down your chin.

That evening I had just come in and I had sat down on the picnic bench, after a date with Nora Kramer, looking characteristically confused and hang-faced, no doubt, wanting consolation and understanding, or at least a Sink Burger, and now Fliegelman was shouting into my face about violins.

"Because there isn't any music there," he shouted. "You hear me?"

"I hear you. But what the hell are you talking about?"

"It's an extended metaphor, for Chrissakes. Don't you know what that is?"

"What?"

"It's what you and Nora Kramer aren't. That's what it is."

"Jesus Christ," I shouted back at him. "You're drunk, Fliegelman. You're from Chicago and you're drunk and you're full of shit."

"Like hell," he said. He sat up straight from the picnic table as if I'd said something which offended him. "It's beer. And I've done all I can for you, Arbuckle. I'm going to go liberate my bladder. It's my right as a citizen." Then he stood up from the table and made his way drunkenly back across the dirt floor toward the rest room, moving through the dense pack of student bodies as if he were some redheaded gnome at a bacchanal.

Well, our generation was full of talk of rights and liberation

·

then and of music too (though more about electric guitars than
of violins), and as it turned out, although I paid no serious
attention to him at the time, Stewart Fliegelman was right about
Nora Kramer and me. There wasn't any music there. Nor much
that resembled liberation. And as for Fliegelman himself, his first
attempt at marriage wasn't exactly Beethoven's *Ode to Joy* either.

FIVE

Jack had been home from the Army for almost two years by the time Nora and I moved to Holt. After graduation in June we were married in Boulder in the Episcopal church. Stewart Fliegelman stood up with me and Nora had a friend of hers as attendant. Then when it was time for Dr. Kramer to escort his daughter down the aisle toward the altar he did so without once looking at her—it was as though he just happened to be passing through the church on his way to work, or as if he were still deep in thought about Milton and Bunyan—and Nora looked lovely too, in her white veil and white dress and with her dark hair pulled away from her face like a young girl's. Afterward, though, perhaps as an offering of consolation to her (for the old man certainly felt she deserved consolation, marrying me), he insisted that we take a week's honeymoon in New York at his expense.

So we flew to New York, attended a play on Broadway, saw the sights, ate in restaurants with male waiters in white jackets standing over us, and we held hands under the table—all as you're supposed to do—and it was in New York that we began those icy exchanges in bed which not only characterized that first week of our marriage but the next eighteen years as well. Then in the middle of that week Nora got sick with something, a summer cold or the flu, so we cut short the time in New York and flew home again. The change in air pressure in the plane caused her ears to pain seriously, I remember, and her face was chalk-white when we walked down the ramp. We stayed that night in Boulder with her father and the next day when Nora felt better we drove the three hours east to Holt. The day after that I went to work at the paper and Nora began to plant rosebushes behind our house in the dirt along the garage. It was not a pleasant beginning for either one of us.

But Jack Burdette seemed to be doing very well. He was home from the Army and it was obvious that he still thought of himself as having had a very good time for those two years while he had been in the service. That is, being a soldier, he had perfected his beer drinking and his poker playing and he had seen something of the nightlife in the towns near the bases he was sent to. Also, he had discovered that money, if he had enough of it, would buy many things that he hadn't known before that it would buy, not excluding the temporary services of other human beings. He told us that he had developed a respectful view of the healing powers of penicillin. We heard all about it once he was home again. There was one story in particular that he told. It involved three German girls and two bottles of champagne and one hotel bed, the kind of arithmetic Jack said he understood. "Them German fräuleins won't refuse you nothing," he said. "You ought to try one yourself."

Thus the Army had served as a kind of finishing school for Jack, a form of postgraduate work in the essential life skills. They had even given him a diploma in the guise of an honorable discharge to prove that he had passed, to show that he had learned their fundamental lessons.

Late in 1962 then, after spending his last paycheck in a final protracted binge, he had returned to Holt. He was heavier and stronger now, beginning to spread out and to take on mass, to develop a heavy gut which daily beer drinking had something to do with, and certainly he was more experienced than he was when he left, but he was probably not any wiser. That didn't matter, though; Wanda Jo Evans was still here and so was his job at the Co-op Elevator. In short time he had taken up both.

In the meantime Wanda Jo Evans had undergone some changes herself. She had reached full bloom now. She had attained a kind of pinnacle of home-grown loveliness. I do not mean that she had become sophisticated in any way; it was not that at all; it was simply that she was even more beautiful than she had been before and that she was still warmhearted and utterly devoted to Jack. At twenty-one she had reached that brief moment of physical perfection. The baby fat was gone, her strawberry blonde hair grew long and full to her shoulders, and now each morning when she walked to work at the phone company she wore nylon hose and heels and a nice skirt and blouse. Consequently it was at about this time that some of the men in town began to make it a point to be drinking coffee at the front tables at the Holt Cafe so they could stare out the windows and watch her walk across Main Street. The men hoped that a sudden gust of wind would rise and lift her skirt to reveal more of her legs, or that a sudden breeze would come up and blow her skirt tighter against her thighs. Failing these, they were there every morning anyway, to watch her mount the curb when she reached the other side of the street. For she was something to see. But she was still a very nice girl, still entirely innocent and guileless, and she herself cared only about seeing Jack Burdette.

When she had begun to earn money as a secretary after she had graduated from high school, she had moved out of her mother's home and had rented a tiny one-bedroom house of her own. It was over there on Chicago Street on the east side of town where there are mainly small one-story frame houses painted white and yellow and sometimes pink, with little gray slap-sided toolsheds in back along the alleys and vacant lots between the

houses, with here and there an old wheelbarrow or an old car, a
DeSoto or a Nash Rambler, say, rusting on blocks among the
pigweed and redroot under the stunted elms. She worked
steadily, efficiently, at the telephone office every day, and she kept
her little house clean, mowed the lawn on summer evenings,
shoveled the snow off the walks in winter, and for two years while
Jack was gone she composed letters to him, following him from
El Paso to San Francisco and then to Germany, all by mail, by
letters—letters which Jack himself only rarely answered and then
only to allow, as he would, I suppose, that he was in California
now or that he had arrived in Germany, or perhaps (and this is
more likely, knowing Jack) simply to complain that he had lost
his weekend pass for some minor infraction of military rules and
so had nothing better to do with his time than to scribble her a
brief note on Army paper while he waited for the other men to
come back so he could begin to play cards again.

But finally in the winter he had returned to Holt once more
and it was all right again. Or perhaps for Wanda Jo it was better
than all right, since for the next eight years she continued to go
out with him, believing all that time that he would marry her yet.

Well, it was an abject kind of love. And it took many forms.
But clean socks was at least one of them.

I think it must have been a matter of barter to Wanda Jo, a
kind of romantic transaction. It was as if she believed that washing
his socks and laundering his shirts was not only the obvious and
logical progression from making crib sheets for him when they
were in high school, but that now doing his laundry each week
was also the fair means of exchange for the privilege of going out
with him on Saturday nights. Because for eight years, Jack would
park his car in front of her house on Chicago Street, on those
Saturday nights, and then he would get out and saunter up to her
house and under his arm he would carry to her front door a brown
paper bag—a bag which would never contain roses or carnations
or even a handful of daisies but which instead would always be

stuffed to overflowing with another week's accumulation of his
dirty clothes, his dirty socks and his greasy shirts. Then Wanda
Jo would open the door to him and take that paper bag from his
hands. It was as if she thought he'd brought her a gift, a present,
a romantic offering, as though she believed he'd given her
something which was actually valuable and considerate. And of
course in return she'd have something to give him too; she'd hand
him that other paper bag, the one with his clean clothes in it—his
sour socks and his old work shirts and his soiled jeans transformed
now, sweet-smelling, washed and tumble-dried and still fragrant
of soap, as though in the intervening week she'd managed to
perform some miracle or magic. And in truth she had: she had
accomplished a kind of domestic and loving alchemy.

Then Jack would say: "Thanks, Wanda Jo." Or he might even
become extravagant; he might say: "Thanks a lot, kid."

So they'd leave her little house on Chicago Street then.
They'd walk out to his car together, with Jack's big arm draped
over her smooth silky shoulder under her strawberry hair, and at
the car Jack would throw the sack of clean clothes into the
backseat. Then they'd go out for the night, to drink at the tavern
on Main Street or to drink and dance at the Legion on Highway
34. It was all a weekly occurrence; it happened every Saturday
night. And afterward, after the bars had closed and after Jack had
told his last joke to the last man still there in the bar who was still
sober enough to laugh in the right places, they would usually go
back to Wanda Jo's house again. Then for an hour or two there
would be another kind of exchange in the back bedroom where,
we understood, Jack would teach her the tricks he himself had
paid to learn while he was in the Army. And none of us doubted
that Wanda Jo was obliging about that too. Because she loved him.
Because she still thought of him as a big black-haired man with
a good sense of humor. She was willing to wait for him for all those
years—for him to make up his mind about marrying her—
because she still believed he would eventually. She hadn't any-

thing else in mind for herself. Jack Burdette was the sum total of
what she hoped for in life. She told me that once.

It was on one of those Saturday nights. It was in March or
April, toward the end of winter, after Jack had been back in Holt
for six or seven years.

I had been working late at the *Mercury* rather than going home
to Nora and a silent house. Nora would be reading as usual,
wrapped up in an afghan in the front room, and Toni, our little
girl, who was two or three then, would already be asleep in her
bed upstairs under a white comforter. So I had gone back to the
office after supper to try to work on an editorial I was writing for
the next week's issue of the paper, and afterward I had walked
up the block to the Holt Tavern on Third and Main streets. I
wanted noise and laughter; I wanted to drink a beer among friends
before going home again. At the tavern I stood at the bar talking
to Bob Sullivan for a while.

Bob Sullivan was a semiretired farmer who had moved to
town recently, and at the moment he was seriously disappointed
in his granddaughter Amy. She had married a local boy named
Jerry Weaver six months earlier. "And the kid wasn't any good
for her," Sullivan said. "I told her so. Here she's just a year out
of high school and then this Weaver kid talks her into a church
wedding before she even has time to turn around good and see
what else there might be in the world waiting for her."

"How old is she?" I said.

"Nineteen."

"It's pretty young to get married."

"That's what I mean." Sullivan said. "But do you think you
can tell these kids that?"

"No I don't."

"Well you can't."

Sullivan ordered another Jack Daniel's on the rocks. After it
was on the bar in front of him he drank half of it at once.

"So," he said, "after I see she's going to go through with it,

I decided: hell, all right, then, I'll make it easier on her. I'll buy her a nice double-wide trailer as a wedding present. And I did. It was brand-new too when I give it to her."

"That was good of you."

"Because you don't think that kid has any money, do you?"

"His family has two or three sections of wheatland. They ought to have some money at least."

"But do they spend it?"

"I wouldn't know."

"They don't. And now I wish I didn't either. I'm going to tell you why."

"I'm still listening."

"Because," Bob Sullivan said, "the last time I go out to Amy's house it was a month ago Sunday afternoon. I sit down at the kitchen table like I usually do and Amy brings me a cup of coffee. And after I've litten a cigarette to smoke with the coffee, she looks across the table at me and says: 'Grandpa,' she says, 'I wish you wouldn't smoke in my house anymore.' 'What?' I say. 'Grandpa,' she says, 'I just would appreciate it if you wouldn't smoke in my house anymore.' 'You would, would you? Well I'll be damned.' 'Because it's a house rule,' she says. 'Is that right?' I say. 'Yes,' she says, 'it is. Jerry and me made up that rule last week after you was here the last time. I'm sorry, Grandpa.' 'So am I,' I say. 'And I'm getting sorrier.' Then do you know what I did?"

"No. But I can guess."

"I stood up and went outside. That's what I did. I drove home again mad as hell about it. And I haven't been back there since. What do you think of that?"

"It sounds pretty sudden to me."

"That's what I think. Because I'd already taken out my lighter and litten my cigarette. It wouldn't be so bad if she had just told me before I'd already litten. But she never."

"She'll probably get over it," I said.

"I don't know. It's been more than a month."

"Give it awhile longer."

"Sure. But do you know what, Pat?"

"No."

"Do you know what the damn hell of it is?"

"No I don't."

"I miss her. That's what the damn hell of it is. I miss Amy. I miss going out there, talking to her and drinking coffee with her. And tomorrow it's going to be Sunday afternoon all over again too."

Then he looked at me and I shook my head. He drank the rest of his Jack Daniel's and afterward he sat there at the bar stirring the ice in the glass with his finger. Finally he stood up very slowly and went back to the rest room.

While he was gone I moved farther down the bar. I ordered another beer. Toward the back, sitting at a table by herself, I saw Wanda Jo Evans. She waved at me and I walked back to her table and sat down in the chair next to her. Jack Burdette was standing over by the pool table talking to a circle of men, heavy, solid, massive, an imposing presence, standing there talking, gesturing with a full glass of liquor in one hand and a cigarette in the other, his face far above those other faces, florid now and animated, his eyes a little bit shiny. The men were all watching him while he talked.

"You're looking lovely tonight, Wanda Jo," I said. "Is that a new dress?"

"Do you like it?"

"Yes. You look terrific." And she did of course. The dress she was wearing was a pale green color, which set off her hair, and it was made of a soft material which fell smoothly from the shoulder down over her breasts and hips. There were little buttons down the front of it.

She smiled. "You don't look so bad yourself."

"I'm losing my hair," I said. "Look at this." I slapped myself on the forehead where my hairline had been. "If I don't quit this pretty soon I'm going to be a walking cue ball."

"Jack's losing his hair too."

"But he's got more to lose. He could transplant some off his chest and nobody'd even notice."

"I'd notice," she said. Then she laughed. She'd drunk enough to be amused by the thought of that. "He *is* awfully hairy, isn't he?"

"He's the missing link," I said.

We looked over at Jack where he stood beside the pool table. He was telling another joke or retelling one of his stories, and the men standing around him were waiting for the punch line. Jack had their complete attention. A barroom and a male audience were Jack's element.

Wanda Jo turned back and began to twist a straw between her fingers. "I saw your wife and little girl on Main Street yesterday," she said.

"Did you?"

"Yes. What's your little girl's name again?"

"Toni."

"Toni. Well she's cute. And she had the prettiest little dress on. I wanted to hug her."

"She's got some of her mother's good looks at least. But she's stubborn as hell. Maybe you could come over and help us out at nap time."

"I would," she said. "Just let me know." She was serious. "Anyway I think you're lucky."

"Oh? I don't know," I said. Because I didn't think of myself as being lucky. Not in marriage anyway. But of course Wanda Jo meant that I was lucky being a father. I would have agreed with her about that. At least at the time I would have. Toni was what kept Nora and me together.

"But I hope to have children myself," Wanda Jo said.

"Do you?" I said.

"Don't you think I'd make a good mother?"

"Of course."

"I think I would. Only it's getting so late. Sometimes I wish Jack would just hurry up and make up his mind. He says he will but then he keeps putting it off."

"That sounds like him."

"Did you know we were going to be married last summer?"

"No."

"We were. I bought a dress and wedding invitations. But Jack decided he wasn't ready yet."

"I don't suppose he was."

Wanda Jo stopped twisting the straw and looked at me. "Of course he will eventually. I have to think that. Otherwise, what else is all this for?"

"He'll come around. He's just not done playing yet," I said. Then I took her hand; I squeezed it and she smiled. But the smile didn't last long; it didn't change anything in her eyes. Afterward she looked unhappy again.

"Let's have another drink," I said.

So we talked about other things for a time and drank another round or two. And in the end Wanda Jo Evans became drunk while Jack Burdette went on talking to his circle of male friends.

Finally I decided to go home. It was after midnight and they were closing the bar. When the lights were turned on Jack came over and put his arm around Wanda Jo and they walked out to his car together. Outside on the sidewalk he said something which made her laugh, but her laughter was too loud and you could hear it along the storefronts, hanging in the air like fog. I stood on the sidewalk and watched them get into the pickup. Then they drove over to Chicago Street.

So it might have gone on indefinitely. It had already gone on that way for most of a decade. Then in 1970 Doyle Francis turned sixty-five and decided he wanted to retire. And Doyle's retirement turned out to be the first in a series of events which ended

•

it for Wanda Jo Evans, although neither she nor anyone else knew it at the time.

Doyle Francis was the manager of the Farmers' Co-op Elevator in Holt. He had been the manager for more than thirty years—for as long as anyone could remember—and he had worked hard and he had performed valuable service. But now he was tired. He wanted out. He wanted to play golf and to see if he could raise asparagus in the garden behind his house. Consequently early that summer he had notified Arch Withers and the other members of the board of directors of the Co-op Elevator that he would retire in the fall, after corn harvest.

In November, then, about two weeks before Thanksgiving, the board invited all of the local farmers who were shareholders in the elevator, and all of the Co-op employees and the mayor and the town councilmen and all of their wives, to a banquet to be held in Doyle's honor at the clubhouse at the golf course east of town. And Nora and I went too, so I could cover the occasion for the *Mercury*. I don't suppose such an event would have received much play in the *Denver Post* or the *Rocky Mountain News* or, for that matter, in any other newspaper along the Front Range, but in Holt, on the High Plains, it was front-page news. It was a matter of local concern to see how Doyle's retirement would affect things at the elevator.

At the banquet there were the usual long rows of tables set up with chairs along either side and there was a head table established up front. For dinner we had the customary roast beef and mashed potatoes and green peas and coffee and a form of fruit cobbler. Afterward we listened to several brief speeches and testimonials. Then a few of the farmers who were present stood up voluntarily—but a little awkwardly too, with their white foreheads shining fresh and clean for the occasion, under the clubhouse lights, with their big calloused hands showing red beyond the cuffs of their suit coats—and once they had stood up they began to tell stories and jokes at

Doyle's expense, stories about Doyle which everyone in attendance had heard three or four times before and in more profane and expansive versions. But it was a success nevertheless. And of course Doyle took all of this good-naturedly. Then Arch Withers, the president of the elevator board, called Doyle up to the lectern so he could present Doyle with a gift. It was a sizable box wrapped in silver paper and a red bow. Everyone was watching him open it, although Withers and the other members of the board who were sitting with their wives at the head table were more than just watching him: they appeared to be beside themselves. There wasn't a straight face among them. But finally Doyle got the silver wrapping off the box and opened it. Peering inside, he looked bewildered at first, dumbfounded; then he grinned and reached inside and held up the contents of the box for all to see. And what he showed us was not the usual pocket watch or a brass pen and pencil set that would gather dust on some desk. No, it turned out that the board had presented him with a good sturdy outdoor hammock to lie in—and a five-year subscription to *Playboy* magazine to read while he was lying in the hammock. Doyle grinned largely. Then he spoke:

"Boys," he said, "I'm afraid you flatter me. The sad truth is, I'm too fat for one and too old for the other."

Everyone laughed. Then one of the board members called out: "Yeah but, Doyle. What we want to know is, which one is it you're too fat for?"

Then people did laugh. They turned to look at Doyle's wife who was sitting at the head table beside Doyle's vacated chair. She was a small plump kindly woman with white hair, and now her face was suddenly red and her hands were playing in embarrassment with a clubhouse napkin. Doyle spoke again:

"Course," he said, "I suppose I could always lose some weight. I mean I might even manage to get skinny again. Don't you think?"

People laughed once more, and when he carried the box over
to his chair and set it down and then bent and kissed his
white-haired wife loudly on one of her red cheeks, kissing her
with obvious good humor and genuine affection even after more
than forty years of marriage, people applauded.

So that much of Doyle Francis's retirement banquet was a
success. People in Holt felt good about it. And I believe they felt
good about the final proceedings that night too.

Because what happened next was the public announcement
that Jack Burdette had been chosen to succeed Doyle Francis as
manager of the Co-op Elevator. Arch Withers made the announcement. Leaning heavily on the lectern, speaking solemnly
to the audience, he said that he and the board recognized that it
would be hard to fill Doyle's shoes, but that they had decided to
look no farther than right here at home. After thinking about it
thoroughly they had come to a unanimous decision; they had all
agreed to promote Jack to manager.

People applauded once more. Everyone approved. And while
Jack walked up the lectern to shake hands with Arch Withers, one
of the farmers in the audience said: "Well at least his feet are big
enough. Burdette ought to be able to fill Doyle's shoes, or anybody
else's, with them big boats."

Sitting in the middle of the room at one of the long tables,
Wanda Jo Evans might have said something about Jack's having
clean socks too. But she didn't—although when I looked at her
there were tears shining in her eyes, tears of love and approval,
I suppose, but also of private expectation. For I think Wanda Jo
Evans must have thought that now, with his promotion, Jack
might want to settle down, that he might be ready to make their
relationship—that almost-eight-year-old Saturday night transaction of theirs—not only a weekly exchange but a daily and
permanent condition.

                  *   *   *

Then it was 1971. It was spring. Jack had been the manager of
the Co-op Elevator for about six months. At the beginning of April
that year the board decided to send him down to Oklahoma, to
Tulsa, so he could attend a weekend convention for the managers
of grain elevators. It was the board's belief that it would be
worthwhile for him, and the elevator too, if he would attend the
convention, sit in on the seminars and workshops, and then return
with the latest predictions about the futures market as well as any
new information he might collect about the prevention of grain
dust explosions. An under secretary of agriculture, several econ-
omists and university scientists were to be there, to lead the
workshops and seminars.

So Jack drove down to Tulsa. He went alone, driving one
of the company pickups with two or three different company
charge cards in his pocket. He left on Thursday. The
convention was to begin at noon on Friday at the Holiday Inn,
and it was understood that he would stay through the
weekend, return on Monday sometime late in the afternoon or
early evening, and then make his report to the board at a
special meeting on Tuesday. And apparently Jack arrived in
Tulsa on Thursday evening just as planned. He found the
Holiday Inn, checked himself into the motel, located the dining
room and the bar, hobnobbed with some of the other elevator
managers, listened to their stories and told some of his own,
went to bed at a reasonable hour, and afterward there is reason
to believe that he even attended some of the meetings on
Friday afternoon and again on Saturday. But by Saturday night,
apparently, he had had enough.

I don't know; perhaps he was just bored. Perhaps he was
tired of it all already. Attending convention workshops and
seminars would no doubt have been too much to him like taking
high-school classes and college instruction. There would have
been all that talk in those close windowless rooms, with the
pitchers of ice water and the urns of coffee set out on a table in

the back, but nothing stronger, nothing for a man to drink really: those experts up at the front of the room talking on and on, speaking learnedly, humorlessly, professionally about corn futures and grain dust explosions, with the accompanying racks of charts and diagrams beside them and the sheaves of documented scientific research, all of which he was not only supposed to believe and make sense of but to take careful notes about too with that ballpoint pen and that new tablet they would have given him, sitting there at some table with his big muscled arms resting out over the table in front of him like two oversized ham steaks while he calculated the hours and minutes until dinnertime and the first drink of the evening, though not necessarily in that order. And meanwhile the experts would still have been talking and he would still have been trying to stay awake. Consequently I believe he must have been good and bored by Saturday night, tired of it all. But also, I know, by that time, he had met Jessie Miller. And Jessie Miller, as she was known then, would have been enough to make him want to disappear even if he weren't bored.

She had been hired by one of the sponsors of the convention to stand behind a table set up in the lobby. She had been instructed to wear a white blouse and a black miniskirt, to smile congenially, to pass out glossy colored brochures, and to show continuously a film extolling the virtues of a particular species of hybrid seed corn. And she had been doing all of this faithfully all of Friday afternoon and all of Saturday. So Jack must have met her, or at least have talked to her, several times already.

Then on Saturday evening, after he had been released at last from the last workshop late that afternoon, he began seriously to charm her. For he was capable of charm. I may not have made that clear, the fact that Jack Burdette could be attractive to women, that he was capable of exercising considerable charm and persuasiveness where women were concerned. Still it's true; on those occasions when it mattered to him what women thought of him and whenever it made any difference to him how they

·

responded to his talk—that is, when he wanted something from a woman—he was in fact capable of great leverage and conviction. But he had that effect on men too. He dominated any room he entered. But it wasn't all conscious and deliberate on his part. Most of it was a matter of impulse and instinct, the result of native vitality and energy. He was full of himself. Domination came naturally to him. And in any case, he was huge, and he still wasn't bad-looking at that time. He hadn't gotten sloppy yet.

So he began to charm her. She was just twenty years old in 1971 and he was already thirty. He wined her and dined her, bought her steak in the dining room and danced with her in the lounge until late that night, swirling her around the floor to the live music played by the country band hired by the sponsors of the convention, and he mixed it all with a variety of expensive wines which he charged on the Farmers' Co-op Elevator's charge cards. Then he disappeared with her. They went upstairs to his motel room and didn't come out until Monday morning—not until everyone else at the convention had already checked out and had gone home—leaving the motel room only then to have their blood tested and afterward to locate the nearest justice of the peace before returning once more to the privacy of Jack's room at the Holiday Inn.

Thus he didn't return to Holt again until late Wednesday night. And when he did return he was already married. He moved Jessie into his old room at the Letitia Hotel, just a block off Main Street.

This surprised and astonished everyone in Holt. But it was more than mere surprise and astonishment to Wanda Jo Evans. To her it was nearly a lethal shock. And it wasn't even Burdette who informed her of the fact that he was married now. On the contrary, she discovered this in the same way that everyone else in Holt did: by hearsay on Thursday morning, after he had returned from Oklahoma and had already spent that first night with Jessie in the Letitia Hotel.

Still Wanda Jo knew that he was going down to Tulsa. She was aware that the board had sent him to the convention. But I don't believe she thought much about it. No one did. It was simply part of his new responsibilities as manager of the elevator. To Wanda Jo, then, it must have been merely that he would be gone for the weekend and that she would miss their weekly dancing and drinking and later their lovemaking in the back bedroom. So perhaps while he was gone she decided to make good use of her time. Perhaps she gave her little house a thorough cleaning; maybe she had a permanent curl put into her hair and did things like balance her checkbook and sew buttons on one of Jack's shirts. Then it would have been Monday and Jack would have been due to come back.

Except that he didn't come back on Monday. He was still in Tulsa on Monday. He was busy. He was occupied. He was having his blood tested. He was pulling strangers in out of the courthouse hallways to act as witnesses, and he was standing up in front of an unknown justice of the peace, promising the twenty-year-old girl beside him whom he had known now for maybe forty-eight hours that he would continue to love her and take care of her, whether they ever got rich or not, whether they managed to stay well or happened to turn sick, till death did them part. So it was late on Wednesday night before he returned to Holt. It was long after midnight and consequently for another night Wanda Jo Evans must have given up waiting for a phone call that didn't come and she must have gone to bed at last, in confusion and wonderment, beginning now to worry. But finally she must have gone to sleep. Then the next day she discovered that he was married.

It was Joyce Penner, one of the women at the telephone office where Wanda Jo worked, who told her. Joyce heard about it in the bakery. About nine-thirty that morning Joyce walked around the corner to Bradbury's Bakery on Main Street, to buy sweet rolls for the women in the telephone office, and by that time people in town were already talking about it. So, as we all heard later, Joyce went back immediately, without even buying the rolls for the women. Reentering the telephone office she leaned over Wanda Jo's desk and said: "Honey, come back to the ladies' with me."

"What's wrong?" Wanda Jo said. "Is something wrong?"

"Just come back to the ladies' with me."

"Well. Something must be wrong," Wanda Jo said.

But Joyce was already walking away from her, past the other women at their desks. Wanda Jo stood up and followed Joyce back to the rest room, to that little square pragmatic space where there is no window, where there is barely room enough for one person and the fan comes on according to code when the light switch is turned on and it makes a tinny noise, and then Joyce locked the door behind them and told Wanda Jo to sit down. "Why?" Wanda Jo said.

"Just do," Joyce said. And then she told her.

So I suppose bad news can be lethal for some people. Especially if it is sudden and unexpected. That is, if you are not used to it, if you have gone along passively, hoping for the best despite all the evidence to the contrary, if you are twenty-nine years old and still believe that a man will marry you simply because you have washed his dirty socks for eight years and have slept with him on Saturday nights during all that time, then I suppose bad news can kill you. In any case it was something like that for Wanda Jo Evans. Because, in a way, Wanda Jo Evans did die that Thursday morning in April. I do not mean that she slit her wrists with a lady's razor that she happened to be carrying in her purse, nor that she did anything so suicidal as to stab herself with a fingernail file. I simply mean that she stopped caring what happened to herself anymore.

It began immediately. For the rest of that morning she sat in

the telephone office rest room, staring at the tiled floor, wiping
her nose on cheap toilet paper, crying quietly, her recently curled
strawberry blonde hair fallen forward about her abashed and
stricken face and her slim white neck bowed and exposed as if she
were waiting for some final blow of some Holt County inquisitor's
ax. All of that—that dreadful individual remorse and despair and
submission—while the fan overhead went on making its maddening little noise and while the other women out in the front
office continued to talk about her and to send a representative
from among themselves every fifteen minutes or so to check on
her. She stayed in the rest room all that morning. Then at noon
one of the women drove her home.

     For the rest of that spring she drank. In the evenings she went
home after work and sat in front of the television, drinking cheap
wine or vodka until she fell asleep. And on the weekends that
spring she went out to the bars in town, going out alone now to
the same places where previously she and Jack had gone together.
Invariably she drank until the bars were closed. Then, in time, she
began to take someone home with her too. She brought them back
to that little bedroom in the house on Chicago Street, and the bed
wasn't even made anymore and the sheets smelled of sweat and
the stale smoke of old cigarettes. But none of that was important
to her now. It was only important to her that he—whoever he
was, and there were a lot of them during those months of late
spring and early summer, and even occasionally more than one
at the same time—it was only important that he do his own
laundry. She insisted on that.

     By June she was a mess. She was completely lost and pitiable.
And people in Holt did pity her too—the women, in particular,
but some of the men as well, when they thought about it. They
all felt sorry for her. But no one knew what to do for her either.
Finally, however, some unexpected help came from the outside.
It came in the guise of a little mousy middle-aged man who wore
horn-rimmed glasses and a white shirt and tie: a Mr. T. Bleven

McGill. He was a telephone company supervisor and it turned out that he had a heart. T. Bleven McGill persuaded Wanda Jo to apply for a transfer to another office. Thus, at the end of June in 1971, she moved to Pueblo. And so far as I know she is there still.

But before she left she did one thing—something which has become a part of Holt County legend too—she delivered that last brown paper bag of clothes to Jack. They were all clean and dutifully laundered of course. In fact they still smelled faintly of soap. She had washed them during that week just prior to the time that Jack had gone down to Tulsa to the manager's convention, and naturally when he returned he hadn't thought to pick them up. Now Wanda Jo presented them to him one afternoon while he was at the elevator office. Bob Thomas and several other men were there too. She didn't say anything to Jack, nor to any of the others. She merely set the bag on the counter, looked at Jack, stared at him, met his eyes, and then swept her glance over the other men. Finally she turned and walked out.

After she had gone Burdette looked inside the paper bag. He recognized the contents; they were his clothes all right, but they had been changed. They had been cut by a razor or by a pair of scissors, sliced methodically, bitterly, into tiny pieces, the biggest of which was no larger than a single square in a checkerboard or a little girl's hair ribbon: all his socks and shirts and pants and underwear. Burdette dumped the things out onto the counter.

"Huh," he said to other men in the office. "You reckon this means we're through? You suppose this means she won't be doing my laundry no more?"

Bob Thomas and a couple of the men laughed.

"But hell," Jack said. "She was a nice girl. Only she always was a little short on a sense of humor."

PART
TWO

SIX

She was the exact opposite of what people in Holt thought she would be. That is, she was the exact opposite of what people in Holt thought she would *have* to be. If Burdette was going to marry her, if he was going to leave someone as beautiful and selfless and long-suffering as Wanda Jo Evans was and then marry someone else, she would have to be something. At the very least she would have to be some husky-voiced Oklahoma version of Jayne Mansfield or Marilyn Monroe.

She wasn't, though. She wasn't like that at all.

Still from the very beginning Burdette himself misled people about her. That Thursday morning in April, after he had come back from Tulsa the night before and had then returned to work at the elevator the next day, he told Arch Withers about her. And what he told Withers at least implied that she was the kind of woman people still expected her to be. Also, since it was from him, from Arch Withers, that people first heard about her and since no one had met her yet or had seen her on Main Street, and wouldn't see her or meet for another three or four hours—not until noon when she would leave the Letitia Hotel and meet Burdette at the Holt Cafe for lunch—for the length of that one morning (which was still the same morning that Wanda Jo Evans was crying privately, miserably, in the telephone office rest room) people in Holt assumed that she would have to be blonde at least, even if she wasn't also brassy and vacuous and loud, a kind of empty-headed lipsticky Sooner starlet.

That Thursday morning back in April, Arch Withers had been waiting for Burdette near the rough plank steps leading up to the elevator office. He was standing on the gravel in the morning sun, leaning up against the fender of his old black pickup, chewing on a flat toothpick and cleaning his fingernails. By the time Burdette arrived at eight o'clock that morning Withers had been waiting for him for nearly an hour. Then Burdette drove up in the company vehicle he had taken down to Tulsa. He got out and walked over to Withers.

"Well," Withers said. "What happened? Did you get tired of motel food and decide it was time to come home again?"

"No. I liked their food all right," Burdette said. "Their beds was satisfactory too."

"So it wasn't that. Well that's something at least. I wouldn't want to think you missed any meals or lost any sleep on our account—just because you finally come back two days after you was supposed to and never called nobody the whole time and never even answered the phone when somebody else tried to call you."

"Arch," Burdette said, "you sound a little upset."

"That so?"

"Yeah you do. And it doesn't become you."

"Then you'll have to excuse me," Withers said. "Maybe I ought to apologize. Because I'm not upset, goddamn it. I'm mad. Just where in the goddamn hell have you been all this time anyhow?"

Burdette told him about Jessie Miller then, about meeting her in the Holiday Inn lobby where she was showing that continuous monotonous film about hybrid seed corn. He told Withers about dancing with her. "She was pretty good-looking too," he said.

"Was she?" Withers said. "Then I guess I'm glad for you. But what the hell's that got to do with anything?"

"Quite a lot," Burdette said.

"How do you mean?"

"Well. I married her."

"What?"

"I married her."

"The hell you did."

"That's right. I'm a old married man now. Like everybody else."

"I'll be a son of a bitch," Withers said. "I thought you had better sense."

Then, as Arch Withers told it later himself, he chewed his toothpick for a while and studied Burdette, looking him up and down as if Burdette were some sudden bump in the evolution of humankind, and not an attractive one necessarily but as if he were a talking mannequin, say, or an enormous and potentially dangerous aberration.

But finally Withers accepted this new fact and went on. He said: "All right, then, so you're married. You married some good-looking girl in Oklahoma. But Jesus Christ, man, didn't you even go to a single meeting we sent you down there to go to?"

"Sure," Burdette told him. "I went to some of them. I went to a goodly number. I didn't meet her till Saturday."

"Then how come you never come back until Wednesday? You was supposed to report to us here on Tuesday."

"I remember," Burdette said. "But you don't expect them to open that office of theirs on the weekends, do you?"

"What office?"

"The one so we could get our blood tested."

"You mean you got married on Monday?"

"That's right."

"But that still leaves Tuesday."

"No it don't."

Withers stared at him.

"Tuesday was our honeymoon," Burdette said. "We was still in bed on Tuesday."

Withers took the toothpick out of his mouth then and threw it away. He said he didn't have any more use for it now. It didn't taste good to him.

Nevertheless he went on once more. "All right," he said, "I guess some kind of congratulations are in order. And I do congratulate you—I wish you both well. Still I'm only going to hope for one thing."

"What's that?"

"I'm just going to hope that this doesn't spoil your good judgment."

"It never has before."

"Goddamn it—you haven't never been married before either."

"That's a fact," Burdette said. "I haven't even been to Tulsa before. It might get to be a habit."

Burdette slapped Withers on the back then. But Arch Withers still wasn't amused. He climbed into his pickup and started it. Through the open window he said: "How *was* your blood anyway? That report you had. It might be of interest to the board."

"Arch," Burdette said, "it was hot. You just wouldn't believe how hot it was." He began to laugh. "And hers was too," he said.

Then Withers drove away, across the gravel out onto the road and over to Main Street to Bradbury's Bakery. For an hour before going home again, before returning to the tractor waiting for him in the half-plowed field which he admitted he had left for too long already over this damned business, he sat drinking black coffee and eating cream-filled doughnuts while he told some of us what he had just heard. He said he believed that Burdette had stopped laughing as he drove away but that he was pretty sure Burdette was still grinning.

"So," one of us said. "He's married now, is he? Well hell's bells."

"Except you mean wedding bells, don't you?" one of the others said.

"No, I don't. I mean, that son of a bitch. I wonder what she looks like."

As a result of all this there was a considerable crowd at the Holt Cafe on Main Street that Thursday noon. People in Holt knew Burdette ate lunch there and they hoped that his new wife would join him. They wanted to see this new woman for themselves. They wanted to examine her and confirm their expectations. By twelve o'clock all of the tables and booths at the cafe were occupied and there was an increasing number of people standing up at the front door waiting for the possibility of a vacated table. Meanwhile the special of the day—Swiss steak and potatoes and green beans and hot apple pie—had already been used up.

Then a little after twelve Burdette walked in. He stood just inside the doorway a moment, scanning the tables and booths, looking across the steamy overfilled room for a place to sit. A couple of the local men waved at him, motioning for him to come join them at a center table opposite the salad bar. He acknowledged the men, but then he walked past their table and over to a booth in the corner. There was a young woman sitting in the booth, alone.

She had come in earlier. I believe she had been there for about thirty minutes; maybe more than that. When she had entered the cafe late that morning people had noticed her—anyone new in town would be noticed—but I don't think they had thought much about it. I suppose they—we—had all assumed that she was just some single woman from out of town who was passing through Holt on Highway 34 and that she had only stopped for lunch and maybe for an hour of rest at the cafe. Still there were people who were annoyed with her too; those men and women who were standing up at the doorway kept glancing at her, indicating by their quick harsh glances that she ought to have the decency to get up and leave. She was occupying an entire booth by herself, a booth which they themselves had more immediate and urgent need of.

Then Burdette did something which surprised everyone in the cafe. He sat down with her—not across from her but beside her—and he put his arm around her. He pulled this new unknown young woman to himself and kissed her.

And suddenly it was as if you could actually hear the insuck of breath from the men and women sitting in the cafe that noon when they realized who she was, when they understood who she had to be. It was like that moment that comes in a movie when everything—music, motion and sense—is stopped for a few seconds and the figures on the screen are held temporarily in silent stasis and arrest. People in Holt felt shocked. She wasn't anything like what they expected her to be. There were some in the cafe who even wondered if she weren't part Indian.

For Jessie Burdette, it turned out, was a very quiet and solitary woman. She had brown eyes and dark brown hair and beautifully clear skin, and she was of less than medium height and she was quite slim, but she wasn't petite. She didn't make you think of girlish debutantes or of retiring primroses. She wasn't even pretty really. That is, she was attractive, she was very attractive; and later, thirteen years later, when I came to know her well I thought she was the most attractive woman I'd ever known and absolutely the finest person. And in the end I was ready to do anything at all for her. Still she was not pretty in any conventional sense. She wasn't at all the positive and cute, sunny little pert-nosed girl next door; nor was she any form of that brash California idea of female pulchritude either. Instead she was rather small and dark and quiet and obviously strong-willed. She seemed capable of a great deal. She seemed independent. Even on that first day, when I saw her for the first time in the Holt Cafe, there seemed to be a quality of aloofness about her, as if she preferred really to be left alone, or as if she knew very well what she wanted and if that happened to preclude being close to others—so that she must always seem a little set off and separate from other people in Holt, or, for that matter, from people anywhere else in the world—she was willing to accept that too.

So I don't know why she married Jack Burdette. Not absolutely, at any rate. On the other hand, as I've suggested before, I think I do know why Burdette married her: out of boredom. He decided that charming Jessie was at least preferable to attending any more convention workshops. Then, too, he had those company charge cards in his pocket. He wouldn't have wanted to waste an opportunity to spend money which did not belong to him, especially if it was simply a matter of having to scribble his name on a piece of paper. But I can't say absolutely why Jessie married him.

I suppose part of it had to do with the fact that she was only twenty years old in 1971. She was still very young, although she was not entirely ignorant of the ways of the world and men. She had had some experience of both, some limited experience. But the point is, she was very young even so. She was not much more than a girl yet. Besides, she had lived her entire life in Tulsa. And I don't think, at twenty, that Jessie Burdette believed that Tulsa was all there was in the world worth seeing.

So in April that year Jack Burdette arrived at the Holiday Inn. He was a big man and jovial, and he was ten years her senior and he was from Colorado. And so he charmed her. And then, rather than return to any more convention workshops, he proposed marriage to her. And, for her own reasons, she accepted. But there was one other little bit of play in this weekend romance too: sometime during those days and nights in the motel room Burdette managed to convey the impression to her that Holt was better than it is. He told her, for example, that you could see the mountains from Holt.

You can't of course. You have to drive at least forty miles west of here to see the mountains. And then it has to be a very clear day, coming after it has rained or after the wind has blown hard for five or six hours so that the brown cloud hanging over Denver has been driven away or been blown off, and then what you see of mountains is merely a faint blue jagged line on the horizon some hundred miles farther to the west. But to Jessie Burdette, as later she would describe the manner in which Jack had told her about it, Holt County would at least have seemed different from Tulsa, Oklahoma. And she thought she had good reason to want out of Tulsa, Oklahoma.

She was the oldest of three children. The two others were boys, younger than she by five and six years. Her mother was an invalid, confined to a wheelchair, and her father was an implement salesman who was gone from home most of the time. As a teenager then, after her mother was crippled, she had spent many hours taking care of her mother and her two little brothers. She knew a great deal about cooking and cleaning and washing clothes and changing bedpans and emptying urine bags, and she had worked part-time in the evenings at fast-food restaurants, and she had even saved a little money to buy material to make clothes for herself. But she didn't know much about fun. It was all a kind of gray reiteration of things to her, an endless unhappy routine. Then she graduated from high school. And after graduation she had worked as a temporary secretary on several occasions. But none of that was taking her anywhere. Then it was about this time that her father, because of business associations, heard about the weekend job at the elevator convention at the Holiday Inn. So she

applied for the job and she was hired to show the film about hybrid
seed corn in the motel lobby. She wore the miniskirt they required
her to wear and the short-sleeved white blouse with the low
neckline, and all the time she managed to smile congenially at the
men at the convention. Then Jack Burdette showed up and began
to talk to her. And soon it was more than just talk, and then on
Monday he married her.

So for the next five years, after seeing her for the first time in
the Holt Cafe that Thursday noon, like everyone else in town I
still only saw her infrequently. And then it was only causally,
remotely, as from a safe and necessary distance. On those occasions when she happened to be shopping on Main Street, or on
those rare weekend nights when she would agree to go out to the
bars with Burdette, I would see her, just as everyone else did, and
pay attention to her.

She was still doing some of that then—going out to the bars,
I mean. During those first seven or eight months after Wanda Jo
Evans had left town and while she herself was still new among us,
we would see her every once in a while at the Legion or at the
Holt Tavern on Saturday nights. And we would all watch her then.
Typically, she would be sitting quietly in a corner booth by herself,
sipping some sugary drink very slowly while the ice in her glass
melted away, thinning the pink liquor to mere colored water,
while Burdette himself (since marriage hadn't changed him; since
marriage was merely a change in his weekend companion, not a
real break in his Saturday night routine, that masculine habit and
custom of his) would be standing off at the end of the bar away
from her, drinking whiskey or scotch, the center of that constant
and admiring group of backslapping men, while he told his jokes
and stories and they all laughed.

That wasn't often, though; we didn't see much of that. Jessie
Burdette did not go out to the bars very regularly. And when she

did go out she was always pleasant and would talk to you if you said something to her, but she would never volunteer anything herself. Instead she seemed to prefer to sit quietly sipping her watery drink, watching others have what she maybe didn't even consider then as being a very good time.

But in the meantime the local women had begun to work on her, to pay special attention to her. I suppose the women in town wanted to be friendly. They began to ask her to join their social clubs and their church organizations. Wouldn't she like to come to tea, to join Rebecca Circle, to play bridge, to be a member of the Legion Auxiliary, to golf with them on Saturday mornings, or maybe—wouldn't she like to participate in Bible study?

But she wouldn't, she told the women. She refused them outright, although when they called on her she was pleasant about it all. Nonetheless she was certain about it too.

So the women felt a little hurt by this, a little bit rebuffed and rejected. It put them off. But a month or two later they decided to ask her again. She only needed more time, they told one another; she was merely being polite. She probably wanted to settle in more thoroughly and to look about her, as anyone would, moving to a new town. With the passage of time, she would feel differently, they said. In the middle of fall that first year they began to ask her again.

But again she refused their invitations, rejecting that female attempt at communal neighborliness and sociability a second time. She hadn't changed her mind at all, it turned out. While we understood that she was still quite cordial to them, in that typical, quiet and pleasant manner of hers, she was also absolutely certain about it. She was not in the least bit interested.

And now the women felt more than a little put off. They were offended. They felt wounded by her rejection. As a result, they stopped asking Jessie Burdette to join anything at all.

*   *   *

Then in March of 1973, almost two years after she had arrived in town, she had a baby. She delivered a little boy whom she named Thomas John. Later, when that became too much of a mouthful, she shortened it to TJ. He was a handsome little boy. He had his mother's dark hair and her sober brown watchful eyes. And it was obvious to us, seeing them on Main Street, what she thought of him. She was delighted with him. We would see them together: the young woman, small and quiet and trim again after her pregnancy, pushing the handsome little boy along the street in a baby carriage, the two of them going in and out of the stores, looking as content with themselves as if nothing else mattered. She would be smiling at him too, talking to him quietly as though he could already understand what she was saying. Then later when he was a little older and when it was summertime we began to see them in front of the house on Gum Street (for Burdette had made a small down payment on a two-bedroom house by that time; it was in the middle of town, near the railroad tracks)—this new mother and her little boy would be playing together on a blanket spread out on the grass in the shade under the elm and hackberry trees. He was a little more than a year old when she delivered a second child.

This one was a boy too, named Robert and called Bobby, who was almost the exact twin of his older brother: a handsome little boy with the same brown hair and the same brown watchful eyes. She was pleased with him as well. She was delighted with both of her sons.

Consequently there were three of them now for us to watch in town. Three of them to notice on Main Street or to observe in the yard in front of the house, playing games on the front lawn or making little farmsteads in the dirt with miniature cows and horses and bits of sticks—this young woman whom nobody knew at all yet, whom we had expected in the beginning to be some playgirl, some Oklahoma Monroe or Mansfield with a heaving bust and a cinched-in waist above wide hips and long legs, but who, it happened, wasn't like that at all.

Thus there developed a kind of mystery about Jessie Burdette in Holt. None of us knew what to think of her. Who was she, really? We didn't know. It was as if she were some fine and exotic bird that had flown in here one spring and had then decided to stay—but one which didn't seem to expect any sustenance or even association from anything or anyone around her.

So for five years she was left almost entirely alone. She was merely here, living in a town of three thousand where everyone knew everyone else. And no one knew her.

Then everything changed, for her and for those of us who were still watching her. It had to do with her husband. Sometime in the middle of the afternoon on the last day of December in 1976 Jack Burdette disappeared. And in the end he did not return to Holt for a very long time, not until a great deal of damage had already been done.

SEVEN

At first people in Holt were not alarmed by his disappearance. On the contrary, they were rather amused by it. They thought of it as a kind of joke, as another of his sudden and outlandish acts which in time would be explained, or at least accepted, as just another installment in that ongoing legend that followed him about the town.

Then he'd been gone for about a week. And it began to get about—in the bakery and the pool halls and the tavern, wherever people were talking—that he had charged some things on Main Street before he left.

We learned that on that Friday afternoon on the last day of December he had gone into Foster's Jewelry Store and after looking at several men's rings and old-fashioned pocket watches he had chosen the most expensive 14-carat gold Bulova wristwatch that Lloyd Foster had to offer. And he hadn't paid for it; he had merely signed his name to a charge slip. Then he walked out of the store with the new gold watch on his wrist and went next door to do the same with Ralph Bird.

And there, at the Men's Store, he charged a new maroon sport coat and a pair of good gray wool slacks, a leather belt and three

long-sleeved oxford-cloth shirts—all of which satisfied Ralph
Bird so well (since Bird hadn't expected to conduct any business
at all in that dead time following the Christmas rush) that he
decided, uncharacteristically, to throw in a good new striped tie
to boot.

And Burdette thanked him. He slapped Ralph on the back and
signed his name to another charge slip. Then he walked out of the
Men's Store wearing the coat and the slacks and the belt and one
of the shirts—with the other things (the two extra shirts and the
bonus tie and his old clothes) all stuffed into a plastic store bag.
Once he was outside, he walked up to the corner to Schulte's
Department Store.

But we discovered that he wasn't quite so successful there.
It happened that old Mrs. Thompson was the only clerk available
at the moment and it was she who waited on him. In no uncertain
terms Mrs. Thompson informed Burdette that the store had
specific limits on how much they would allow anyone to charge.
Burdette took this amiss. "But look here," he said. "You know
me. You know who I am."

"I certainly do," Mrs. Thompson told him. "I've heard more
about you than I ever want to, ever since you were an ornery little
boy. Your mother is a friend of mine."

Consequently, at Schulte's, Burdette was somewhat ob-
structed in his Friday afternoon shopping; that is, he was allowed
to charge only a pair of dark socks and a set of blue underwear.
And before he left the store he must have thought better of
changing into the socks and the underwear and wearing them out
onto the street. Mrs. Thompson was still watching him.

Despite these new stories about Burdette which everyone in
town heard and afterward repeated, people in Holt were still not
alarmed. They were still amused by his disappearance and by his
post-Christmas shopping spree. If nothing else, there was a good
deal of joking and fun to be had at Lloyd Foster's and Ralph Bird's
expense. People said that either man could profit by hiring Mrs.

Thompson to clerk in his store. They said Mrs. Thompson would at least have cut their losses.

But then that first week of Burdette's disappearance turned into a second week. And then gradually the jokes in the bakery and the pool halls and the tavern began to grow stale and there began to be other people in Holt, besides Ralph Bird and Lloyd Foster, who were growing doubtful that Burdette was ever going to return. No one had any idea where he was and there wasn't anyone in the county who could imagine what was keeping him away.

It was the middle of January then. It was late on a Friday afternoon and it was at this time that Jessie Burdette came into the office of the *Holt Mercury*. During the afternoon it had been snowing and now it was very cold outside. There was little traffic on Main Street and the wind was blowing the dry wisps of snow along the sidewalk. Above the storefronts it was beginning to turn dark.

Jessie Burdette came into the *Mercury* just before five o'clock. She had the two little boys with her. TJ was almost four years old then and Bobby was almost three. They came in bundled up in their winter clothes, the boys in matching snowsuits and Jessie in a navy blue wool coat which was still loose enough that she could button it over her stomach; for, although we didn't know it yet, she was pregnant again; she was already in her fourth month. Inside the office she sat TJ and Bobby down together on a wooden chair against the wall. The little boys looked handsome as ever and red-cheeked. She unzipped their snowsuits and smoothed the hair back from their foreheads. "Now sit still, please," she told them. Then she stepped up to the counter and waited for Mrs. Walsh.

Mrs. Walsh was the office receptionist. My father had hired her to work in the office twenty years earlier as copy editor, and she had stayed on all those years although my father himself had

retired in 1970 and had left the daily management of the paper
to me. Now she stood up from her desk and approached the
counter. From across the room I watched her talking to Jessie
Burdette.

"Yes?" Mrs. Walsh said. "Can I help you?"

"I want to print something in the paper."

"Is it an ad?"

"No. It's not an ad."

"Ads are fifty cents per line."

"It's not an ad, though."

"What is it, then? Do you have it with you?"

I watched Jessie reach into her coat pocket and draw out a
sheet of yellow tablet paper. She began to unfold it on the counter.
When it was completely unfolded she pushed it across the counter
toward Mrs. Walsh.

Mrs. Walsh picked it up and held it close to her face under
the light. Immediately she put the paper down again. She stood
up very straight. "Why," she said, "we can't print this. This is . . .
We can't print this."

"I intend to pay for it," Jessie said. "Is that the problem?"

"No that is not the problem."

"What is the problem, then? Why can't you print it?"

"It's simply unprintable."

Jessie looked past Mrs. Walsh, looking across the room at
Betty Lucas who was typing at her desk, and then at me. "Is there
someone else I can talk to?" she said.

"What?"

"I'd like to talk to someone else, please."

"But they'll just tell you the same thing I have."

"What about Mr. Arbuckle? He's the editor, isn't he?"

"Mr. Arbuckle is busy."

"I'd like to talk to him."

"But I've just told you. He's busy."

"Yes, but would you ask him to come over here?"

I stood up from my desk and walked across the room to the counter. Mrs. Walsh had begun to shake. The dark veins at the side of her head stood out beneath her white hair. "Is there something wrong, Mrs. Walsh?"

"This young woman thinks we will publish this in the paper."

"What is it?"

"Here," she said. "You read it. I refuse to." She handed the tablet paper to me.

"Thank you, Mrs. Walsh," I said. "Maybe you can begin closing up now."

She turned and sat down at her desk. I could hear her behind me. She was upset. She had begun to whisper in the direction of Betty Lucas.

I read what was on the paper. It was a brief notice. It had been written in pencil and the paper it had been written on had been folded many times, into small squares, and at the edges it was frayed and ragged as though she had been carrying it around in her pocket for a week waiting for the right moment to bring it in. Then I looked at Jessie. Her eyes were very brown and her cheeks were still red from having been outside in the cold. I thought she looked very beautiful. There were bits of dry snow on the shoulders of her blue coat.

"Yes," I said. "I've heard your husband was gone. I suppose we've all heard that much. But I take it you haven't heard from him yet either. Is that what this is about?"

"No. I haven't heard from him."

"Where do you think he is?"

"I don't know. I haven't any idea where Jack Burdette is."

"You've notified the police, though?"

"Yes. But yesterday there was a bill in the mail."

"A bill?"

"For some clothes he charged," Jessie said. "So I called them back and told them they could stop looking for him. He isn't lost."

"I see," I said. "I think I do, anyway." Because it seemed

obvious to me now, having read what she'd written on the piece of tablet paper, that she had come to a thorough understanding about the charges Burdette had made on Main Street and also about what those charges indicated about his disappearance. She hadn't had to be present for the jokes and the talk in the bakery, or later to be there to hear the growing alarm people felt. She seemed to understand all too well what those things would mean to her as his wife in Holt.

I looked outside for a moment. On Main Street it was fully dark now. The streetlights had come on and it was snowing again. Behind me Mrs. Walsh and Betty Lucas had begun to put their coats on, preparing to go home for the evening. I waited until they had gone out through the back room into the alley. Then I turned back to Jessie.

"I wonder, Mrs. Burdette," I said, "I wonder if you don't think this is a little bit drastic? After all he might come back. Don't you think? Maybe he's just taking a vacation."

"No," she said. "I don't think that. I've stopped thinking that. It's been two weeks."

"Yes. But two weeks aren't a lifetime."

"They're long enough."

"And so you still want me to print this in the paper? You do want that?"

She began to open her purse. "How much is it?"

"But wait a minute," I said. "I haven't said I will yet."

She looked at me. Her eyes were very large and dark. I picked up the penciled notice once more, reading it again while she turned to see that the two little boys were still seated quietly on the chair behind her. They were watching her like little birds.

Finally I said: "Very well, then. I'll agree to print this. Although I don't think it will do you any good. In fact I'm afraid it will do you a great deal of harm in town."

She still wanted it printed. So I took out a form from a shelf

·

under the counter. I copied her note onto the form as she had written it and afterward she paid for it.

She began to prepare TJ and Bobby to go outside again. They sat solemnly in front of her while she knelt to zip up their snowsuits; she helped them pull their mittens on.

I was standing behind the counter, watching her. Her blue coat was smooth and neat across the hips and her hair looked dark and lovely. "Listen," I said, "will you let me drive you and your boys home? I'm leaving now anyway."

She looked out the front window. Outside it was worse: it was snowing harder and the wind was blowing the snow horizontally along the street. "If it's not any trouble," she said. "I don't want them to get cold again."

"I'll get my coat."

Thus she allowed me to drive them across town to Gum Street that first time because it was snowing and because it was cold outside. I don't recall that we said anything of significance. TJ sat on the seat between us and she had Bobby on her lap and I suppose during the six- or seven-block ride one of us managed to say something about the accumulation of snow. It was a quiet and awkward ride. But at the curb when I stopped to let them out I remember watching her take the boys up the sidewalk into their small house in the snow and I recall how she looked in her blue coat when she opened the door and then how the house itself looked after she had turned the lights on. Afterward I drove home again to the house where Nora and Toni were waiting for me to eat supper with them. But I wasn't very much interested in supper just then, nor in going home again, nor even in my wife and daughter. I suppose by that time I was already a little in love with Jessie Burdette.

So in the following week I ran her notice as a kind of display ad on the back page of the *Holt Mercury* just as she had wanted it. I offset it with the announcements for Sunday church services and the obituaries for two longtime Holt County residents. Her notice said: *I'm not responsible for whatever Jack Burdette did or will do. He's no good. It doesn't matter what people say. He's a son of a bitch and I don't care anymore.*

I had my own reasons for printing it.

This public declaration of hers caused a stir in town when people read it. My father, for one, called me on the phone and said I was crazy to print such a thing. What did I think I was doing? It was unprofessional, he said; it was bad business practice. This was Holt County, Colorado, not San Francisco, California. Did I think he'd turned the paper over to have it ruined?

Of course other people in town felt similarly, as I knew they would, although their annoyance and their objections had more to do with moral considerations than with any concern over practical issues. Some of the older women were particularly incensed: they wrote letters to the editor about the appearance of profanity in the *Holt Mercury*. They didn't like it, not the profanity nor the public display of raw emotion, and a number of the women canceled their subscriptions as a result.

Nonetheless, the commotion Jessie's notice caused in Holt County that week was soon forgotten. It was a minor episode compared to what happened in the weeks and months that followed. And all of that got into the paper too.

Then there was one other small event which reflected on what was printed in the *Mercury* at about that time. It was in a minor key. It had to do with Jack Burdette's mother.

She was an ancient woman now, gray-haired and very thin and even more severe than she had been before, but still living alone in the house on North Birch Street and still attending the Catholic church on Sunday mornings when she was able. After her son had been gone for about a month, in a kind of desperate form of masculine absurdity—since no woman would have even

considered such a thing—several of the men in town decided that
they would call on old Mrs. Burdette to ask her some questions.
They thought it would be worthwhile to inquire if she had heard
from her son. They hoped, if nothing else, that she might be able
to suggest where he had gone.

So one afternoon they walked up onto the front porch and
rang the doorbell. But after Mrs. Burdette had opened the door
to them she didn't ask them in. She merely waited inside, in the
dark front hallway of the house, listening to their questions and
foolish talk from beyond the scarcely-opened door. They continued to explain to her what they had come for. Then they
stopped talking; she hadn't said anything yet. She had simply
stared at them out of those clean little wire-rimmed glasses while
she studied one face and then another. She didn't seem to know
or even to care what they were talking about. In exasperation, one
of the men said to her: "But, Mrs. Burdette, look here: you do
know Jack's gone, don't you? You do read the local newspaper?
Why, it's been in the *Mercury*. Haven't you seen it?"

When she spoke finally, her voice sounded harsh and rusty,
as if she hadn't used it in days. "I don't know anything about your
newspapers," she said. "And I don't want to. I read the Bible."

Then she shut the door in their faces. They could hear her
locking it. Afterward they could hear the faint sound of her steps
retreating into the interior of the silent house. So the men were
left standing on the front porch. They felt foolish. They looked
at one another and moved quickly down off the porch like little
boys who had done something silly.

In any case, by the end of January the alarm in Holt had turned
at last to shock and fear. People had finally grown afraid that
something serious had happened to Jack Burdette and they were
disturbed to think so. They still liked Burdette and thinking
something bad had happened to him made them feel less secure

for themselves in their corner of Colorado. The police had begun
to send out all-points bulletins across the state, hoping that might
turn him up. But nothing did. Burdette had disappeared without
a trace.

Meanwhile at the Farmers' Co-op Elevator things were a
mess. Without Burdette there to manage the elevator every day,
nothing was getting done properly and Arch Withers and the
other members of the board of directors didn't know what to do.
Finally they decided to ask Doyle Francis to come back. They
wanted Doyle to run things again, on a temporary basis, so that
the routine shipment of corn and wheat might continue once
more, until Burdette turned up, or until . . . well, until they had
to hire his replacement. Still they refused to think it would come
to that.

Then, about the middle of February, that private feeling of
shock and fearfulness in Holt turned suddenly to hostility and
public outrage. For, by that time, Doyle Francis had had sufficient
opportunity to examine the books at the elevator. And in going
over the books he had discovered that something was wrong. He
called a special meeting of the board to tell them about it. It was
on a Tuesday afternoon.

"Jesus Christ," he told the men when they were assembled
before him in his office. "What in the goddamn hell were you boys
thinking of anyhow?"

"What do you mean?" Arch Withers said.

"Didn't you even check on him? Didn't you even think to
look at these books yourselves?"

"Of course we did. We looked at them. Charlie Soames went
over these books every year with us. So did Jack Burdette. What's
wrong with them?"

"Plenty," Doyle said.

"Like what, for instance?"

"Like this, goddamn it." Doyle pointed to the books spread

out before him on the desk. "As near as I can tell, you're missing about a hundred and fifty thousand dollars. That's what's wrong with them."

"What? Hold on now. You mean to say——"

"I mean that's just an old man's estimate. It's been going on for three or four years."

"What's been going on? What are you talking about?"

Doyle explained it to them. In careful, rational detail, he showed the men sitting across from him what had happened, how the books had been manipulated, how they had been juggled by someone who knew what he was doing. But just a little at first, Doyle said, pointing to the pages of neat figures, then in larger and larger amounts as the months passed. And all very cleverly, in a kind of sleight of hand, as a CPA might do it if he had in mind to do something neat and criminal. Doyle said it had taken him days to understand how it had been done. Finally he had, though. "Oh, it was careful," he said. "I'll give them that much."

The men sat silently, looking at the opened books on the desk. They picked at their hands and refused to look at one another. For his part, Doyle Francis sat back in his chair watching them.

At last Arch Withers said: "All right. If what you say is true, who did it? Who's them?"

"What?"

"You said them. Who do you mean by that?"

"Who do you think I mean?"

"How the hell do I know? Do you mean Charlie Soames?"

"Why not? Charlie did the books, didn't he? He did the books when I was here before and I assume you boys kept him on after I left."

"That son of a bitch," Bob Wilcox said. Wilcox was the young man on the board. "Goddamn that old——"

"And Burdette?" Withers said, interrupting him. "What about him? Was he in on this too?"

"Of course he was. Don't you think he had to be? Why else was he going to charge those new clothes on Main Street and then disappear and not come back home again?"

"By god," Wilcox said. "He's another son of a bitch. We ought to—"

"Shut up," Withers said. "It's too late for any of your hysterics."

"That's right," Doyle said. "It's too late for a lot of things. Except I believe that Charlie's still in town, isn't he?"

"He's still in town."

"Then I'll go get him, if none of you will. I'll bring that—"

"Damn it," Withers said. "I already told you to shut up. Now do it." Young Bob Wilcox started to say something more, but Withers turned and stared at him. Then Wilcox closed his mouth tight and Withers turned back to Doyle Francis. "So what do you suggest we do about this? You seem to of thought about it."

"Oh yes. I've thought about it," Doyle said. "It's about all I have thought about for the last two weeks."

"So? Are you going to tell us what to do or not?"

"There's only one thing to do. We let the sheriff's office handle it now. We call Bud Sealy and tell him to go over to Charlie Soames's house and arrest him and lock him up and then we wait for the trial. What else is there?"

"But there's still the money, isn't there? What about the money?"

"What about it?"

"Well goddamn it. It was our money. It was all us shareholders' money."

"Sure it was," Doyle said. "And you can tell that to the judge too, when you get the chance. But I don't suppose that will get it back for you. Jack Burdette's been gone for a month a half and god only knows where he's gone to. But wherever he is, he's already begun to spend it. You can count on that."

There was silence again while this new thought sank in. The

men stared hatefully at the accountant's books on Doyle's desk. After a time, Arch Withers roused himself once more.

"Go on, then." he said. "What are you waiting on? Make your goddamn call. Call Bud Sealy."

"No," Doyle Francis said. "I don't think I will. I think one of you boys ought to be able to call him. It's your funeral. I've been thinking about this mess for too long already."

So Arch Withers, as president of the Farmers' Co-op Elevator's board of directors, called Bud Sealy from the manager's office that Tuesday afternoon, with the books still spread out on the desk before him and while Doyle Francis and the other men watched him.

And subsequently that same afternoon Bud Sealy arrested Charlie Soames at his home in the six hundred block on Cedar Street, where Soames had a small office at the back of the house. Sealy drove over to the house, parked and knocked on the door. He was let in by Mrs. Soames. She was an excitable old woman with heavy breasts and meaty arms. She led the sheriff back to Charlie's little office and stood in the doorway.

When Sealy entered the room—it was all neat and tidy as ever—Charlie Soames seemed to be waiting for him. He was sitting at his desk with his hands folded and he seemed to have everything in order. It was as though he had prepared himself for Sealy's arrival, as if he were glad that it was over now. "So you know," Soames said.

"Yeah. I just got a call from Arch Withers."

"It took them long enough. I expected you a month ago."

"I'm here now. Are you ready?"

"Yes."

"Ready?" Mrs. Soames said. "Ready for what?" She was still standing in the doorway, displacing air. Her hair stood out from her pink head. "Where are you taking him?"

"Your husband's got himself into trouble."

"My husband? What do you mean? What could he do?"

"Enough," the sheriff said. "Now maybe you'd better go into the other room for a minute."

"I'm not going into the other room. So he has done something. The old fool! He's done something and now what am I supposed to do?"

"For one thing," Sealy said, "you're going to be quiet."

"I didn't do anything. You can't tell me in my own house to—"

"Yes. You're going to be quiet. Or I'm going to gag you."

Mrs. Soames glared at the sheriff. "You wouldn't touch me. You wouldn't dare touch a lady."

"Try me," he said. He took a step toward her and she backed up.

"Oh!"

Then she began to shriek. Sealy shut the door on her. They could hear her excited noises. But after a moment the noises stopped.

"That's better," he said. He turned back to her husband.

Charlie Soames was still seated silently at his clean desk. It was as if he had been waiting for this too. Now he stood up and Sealy told him he had the right to remain silent. Then he put handcuffs around Soames's thin wrists. Afterward they walked out of the tidy little office and on through the house. Mrs. Soames was waiting for them in the dining room; she followed the two men toward the front hallway. When they stopped at the door so the sheriff could open it, Mrs. Soames began to shriek again. She rushed her husband and began to slap at him, at his face and neck. Soames fell down under her hands. She slapped at his head. Finally Bud Sealy shoved in between them, pushing Mrs. Soames away.

"Quit that," he said. "What do you think you're doing? Goddamn it, stop that now."

He lifted the old man by the arm and they went outside. Mrs. Soames followed them out onto the front porch. She stood watching angrily as the car drove away.

When they arrived at the courthouse Sealy walked Charlie Soames down to the basement to the sheriff's office and booked him for the suspected embezzlement of Co-op funds. Afterward he fingerprinted him and then he led Soames back to a cell. He stood over him while the old man sat down on the cot. Soames looked very small and tired. But he wasn't quite defeated yet.

"Well," the sheriff said. "You want to tell me about this?"

"What's there to tell?

"Oh there ought to be something."

"Do you mean you want a formal confession?"

"Something like that."

"What do you want to know?"

"Well. For starters—I'm just curious—why in hell didn't you take off too? You had your chances, didn't you?"

"You mean why didn't I leave?"

"Sure. Like Jack Burdette did. You and Burdette were in this together, weren't you? Why didn't you jump up and leave when he did? You could of left with him."

"Him," Charlie Soames said. The mention of Burdette seemed to awaken something in him. He sat up straight, agitated now. "Why that man . . . that—"

"What about him?"

"He didn't even tell me he was leaving. We agreed on it. He promised me. He wasn't supposed to leave yet. Then he—"

"Sure," Sealy said. "Then he."

"But you don't understand."

"Don't I?"

"No. Because we were waiting for it to amount to two hundred thousand. That's why. And I kept telling him we ought

to leave now. I told him we have to take it and get out now. Before
the auditors find out, I said. They were getting suspicious. I could
tell that. I knew they were. I tried to tell him. But my god, that
man kept saying: 'Just another fifty. Just another fifty.' Like it was
play money or something. Oh, he didn't understand the risks. He
didn't understand anything. And it was his idea from the beginning. I let him talk me into it. But I was the one that had to do
the books, wasn't I? Not him. And he kept promising me: 'Wait
until it's two hundred thousand, then we'll leave together.' That's
what he said. We agreed on that. He promised me. But then
he—"

"Yeah," Sealy said. "Well. You poor dumb old son of bitch.
So he didn't tell you he was leaving either."

"I thought I could trust him."

"Of course. Except you weren't the only one in town that
thought that, now were you?"

"I trusted him, though. And what was I going to do now?
Where was I going to go? He had the money. He took everything.
He withdrew it all out of the bank over in Sterling. And—"

"Sterling? You mean you kept the money over in Sterling?"

"That's where we had our account. I thought it would be
safer. But I still thought I could trust him. I still believed he was
trustworthy."

"That's right," Sealy said. "Because he promised you. Because
you agreed on it."

Soames stopped talking for a moment. He looked at the
sheriff.

"But wouldn't you have said he could be trusted? Didn't you
think Jack Burdette was a trustworthy man?"

"I don't know," Sealy said, "Probably. But I might of said the
same thing about you too, Charlie. And now look at you. Jesus
Christ, look how you turned out."

                    *   *   *

By evening everyone in Holt County knew about the arrest of Charlie Soames. They had heard about the embezzlement of Co-op funds and about his three-year involvement in it. So the panic and outrage had already begun. The Co-op Elevator was owned in shares by half the people in the area and they all wanted blood.

They would have preferred Jack Burdette's and Charlie Soames's blood, both, but Burdette had disappeared. Burdette was already in California, lost somewhere in the streets of Los Angeles. The police had finally managed to trace him that far, but then they had lost track of him. Consequently people in Holt began to understand that they were going to have to content themselves with the arrest of his accomplice, with the indictment and conviction of old Charlie Soames, and then with his rightful punishment. They expected to get something satisfying out of him at least.

And that was awful, really. Charlie Soames was already seventy years old by that time. Like Jack Burdette, he had grown up here. And everyone knew him just as they thought they had known Jack Burdette, except that Soames hadn't any of Burdette's flair for sudden and outlandish acts. He was merely an old man who had always lived here. He had spent his entire life being steady and normal and unremarkable. For almost half a century he had been a bookkeeper and accountant for various businessmen in town, and at forty he had married a woman who was only a year or two younger than he was, a woman who dominated him completely, and together they hadn't been able to have any children. Or perhaps they hadn't even tried to have children. No one knew about that. His wife liked to talk, but that didn't happen to be one of the topics she liked to talk about. No, the truth was, Charlie Soames's entire life had been about as gray as a man's life can be. Now suddenly he had done this.

So he was arrested. And in very short time he was indicted. Then he posted bail and he was released to await the trial. He

made the bail payment out of his own meager life's savings, out
of money which he had accumulated over years of frugality; it had
nothing to do with the embezzlement; he had earned this particular money by doing bookwork for others—the police had
checked. So he was released and then he went home again to his
wife. But that must have been worse than sitting in a cell in the
basement of the Holt County Courthouse on Albany Street. He
would have been left alone for a few hours in jail. There would
have been silence there. But now, once he was home again, Mrs.
Soames must have made it hot for him. She was capable of that.
She must have ground him like hamburger.

Perhaps that was why, about a week after he was released,
he showed up on Main Street once more. It was in the middle of
a weekday morning. He walked into Bradbury's Bakery to have
coffee. I don't know, perhaps he had in mind to test the water,
to take a kind of reading of Holt County feelings about things. The
bakery was crowded as usual at that time of day. Businessmen and
housewives and store clerks and one or two farmers were drinking
coffee and eating doughnuts, sitting about the room at the various
tables. They were all talking.

Then Soames walked into the bakery and everyone got quiet.
They watched this small tidy familiar old man fill his coffee cup
at the urn at the front counter, watched him pay for it and then
turn to find a seat. Across the room there was a vacant chair at
a table near the wall. Ralph Bird and a couple of other men
happened to be sitting at the table. Soames approached them.

"Wait just a goddamn minute," Ralph Bird said. "Where do
you think you're going with that?"

Soames stood beside the table staring at him.

"Get the hell out of here. You ain't sitting here with us."

Soames looked at the other men. He had done books for each
of them. They stared back at him.

And he was just an old defeated man now and he knew
everyone in the room. His hand began to shake. The coffee in the

cup spilled out over his hand and shirt cuff and dripped onto the floor. He was making a mess. He continued to stand there, his hand shaking and the hot coffee burning his hand, while his eyes clouded over. His eyes seemed to lose their focus.

At last one of the girls came out from behind the counter and removed the cup from his hand. "Here," she said, "give me that." It was as if he were a child. She wiped his hand with a dishrag and knelt to wipe the floor.

Then Soames looked once more at the people in the bakery. They were still watching him. He turned and walked out of the store onto the sidewalk. They could see him through the plate-glass windows. He stood for a moment, looking up and down the street. Finally he went home again.

At his home on Cedar Street he entered by the front door and climbed the stairs to the attic. His wife was at the back of the house, peeling carrots at the kitchen sink. Later she would tell people that she didn't even know he was home yet. He was always so quiet.

She did hear the explosion in the attic, however. Several other people did too. The neighbors heard it.

Because, after he had mounted the stairs, he had entered the dusty box-filled room and had sat down on an old trunk near the chimney, under a single dim light bulb suspended from one of the rafters. Sitting on the trunk, he had put a shell in the chamber of an old .22 single-shot rifle. Then he had placed the butt of the rifle on the floor between his feet and had closed his tired little mouth around the gun barrel. And whether he paused once to look about him, as people do in movies, to take one last look out the attic window toward the tops of the trees standing up in the backyard, no one knows. We simply know that he fired a single sphere of lead up through his palate into his brain and that this little sphere of lead destroyed him.

It destroyed him, but it didn't kill him. The bullet had lodged in his brain in such a way that he was still alive.

He was slumped against the chimney when his wife ran upstairs to find out what had caused the noise. The gun was still between his knees. There was considerable blood running down onto his shirtfront and his head was thrown back horribly. He was still breathing, though. There were red bubbles coming up out of his mouth. Looking at him, Mrs. Soames became hysterical. She began to scream. Then the neighbors arrived and it was one of them who called the police.

They flew him immediately to a hospital in Denver. And in Denver the surgeons did what they could; they closed the hole in the roof of his mouth and made other repairs. But in the end they decided to leave the bullet where it was. They said it might kill him to try to remove it. Afterward when he was well enough to be released from the hospital he was brought back home again to Holt.

And so he looked all right, more or less, when we saw him again. He still resembled himself; he was still a neat tidy little old man. It was only his eyes that looked different. His eyes appeared to be blank now, expressionless, as if there was nothing behind them. He could eat and he could drink liquids. He could still function. He could even talk a little, in a harsh lisping monotone. But it didn't matter if he could talk. What he had to say now was all nonsense, mere jabber and repeated dribble about nothing.

So old Mrs. Soames didn't know what to do with him then. She dressed him and fed him every day, and sat him on the swing on the front porch. And occasionally she stood him out in the front yard where he could hold a garden hose in his hands. But, if she let him, he would stand there all afternoon, slapping water on the grass. He seemed to like playing with water. Then people would walk by the house and see him. And sometimes they would say something to him, something cruel and nasty, something vindictive like: "You old son of a bitch. Why don't you try it again? Why don't you use a deer rifle this time? Just try it once. Oh,

·

goddamn you, anyway." And Charlie would simply go on spraying the grass with water while some of it ran off his elbow onto his shoes; he would nod and jabber at the people passing by and he would seem to listen to their talk, cocking his head like some ancient, confused little bird. And when they moved away down the street he would even seem to follow them with his blank eyes. But none of that meant anything to him. It was all a mere show to him, a display of shadows that happened to move and talk. None of it held any significance.

If he had only known it then, I suppose he might even have been happy. He couldn't understand anything his wife or anyone else in Holt had told him, and he couldn't recall the first thing about debits and credits and about double entry bookkeeping. Consequently he knew nothing at all, nothing whatsoever, about his involvement in the embezzlement of Co-op funds.

So he was in a perfect state now: he was mad. He couldn't be bothered anymore and he was completely beyond the reach of the law. There wasn't any way to punish him for what he had done. He was beyond all of that. Any thought of putting him on trial was out of the question.

EIGHT

Now people in Holt felt they had to turn elsewhere for some form of restitution. They felt doubly cheated. Burdette had disappeared at the end of December and every day he was gone it became more obvious that the police were never going to locate him and bring him back. Now his accomplice wasn't even going to be put on trial.

So in time people began to turn on his wife, on Jessie. They wanted satisfaction from someone and she was still here, she was still in Holt, and it made it easier that they thought of her as an outsider. She had been in Holt for almost six years, but she had always been too aloof for her own good, people said. From the day she had arrived she had held herself apart. It was as if she felt she were too good for them—that's what people thought. So they were naturally a little in awe of her, and a little antagonistic. They didn't understand her; they thought of her as that woman Jack Burdette had discovered in some Holiday Inn in Oklahoma, that small quiet overly independent woman he had met and married in Tulsa when he should have married Wanda Jo Evans, a local girl whom everybody liked and admired. No, she had not grown up here, and there wasn't anyone in town who knew very much about her.

So perhaps it was inevitable, given the pitch of emotion and the nature of people, that since there was no one else in Holt who was still available to them, they turned on Jessie Burdette. They were outraged by what had happened and nearly everyone had been affected by it in some way. They began to associate the problems at the elevator with Jessie's arrival. The notice she had printed in the *Mercury* ended up not making any difference to anyone. Too much had happened since then, and now no one quite believed her.

Thus for three or four months that spring Jessie Burdette became public property. There was a kind of general insanity in Holt, a feeling that almost anything was possible. It was as if people had declared open season on her and thought of it as a matter of community honor.

At first there didn't seem to be anything you could put your finger on. There seemed to be merely an increased watchfulness whenever she was present, an intensified correctness and communal coolness toward her whenever she appeared on Main Street. People talked to her now only when they had to, at the checkout stand in the grocery store, or at the gas station when she paid for gas. No one voluntarily greeted her.

Then one evening someone in a car ran over TJ and Bobby's orange cat in the street out in front of the house. The little boys found it the next morning on the front step. Its death might have been an accident but whoever had killed it had brought the cat to the house without stopping to apologize or to offer any explanation. The cat was badly mangled; its fur had been torn open, exposing its insides, and it had been placed where Jessie and the boys were sure to see it. The boys were badly upset by this. Jessie helped them bury it beside the fence in the backyard.

Still, despite this increasing hostility, she continued to stay in Holt. I am not certain why that is, even now. Most of us, I think,

would not have stayed here even for a week, not if we felt we had
any alternative. But perhaps that had a good deal to do with it,
the fact that she felt she had nowhere else to go. There was
nothing for her in Oklahoma anymore; her parents had divorced
and now her mother was in a home for invalids and she hadn't
heard anything from her father in years. She wasn't even certain
where he was. As for her brothers, they had both enlisted in the
military as soon as they had graduated from high school, so she
couldn't have gone to them even if she had wanted to. And in any
case, she didn't want to. She seemed to want to stay in Holt, to
see this out for her own reasons. It was as if she were determined
to react even to these events in her own quiet and independent
way, as if her opinion of herself depended upon this alone. It was
as if she were trying to prove something.

So it was tragic finally. In the end it became more than just
a matter of money. When it was over it was so painful to think
about that there were very few people in Holt who ever wanted
to remember it.

It began in April. At the beginning of April that year she appeared
one afternoon at the elevator beside the railroad tracks. She
walked up the plank steps into the outer office and scale room
and told Bob Thomas she wanted to see Doyle Francis. This
surprised Bob Thomas. It was just after lunch and Bob had eaten
too much as usual and was half asleep. He was slouched at the desk
behind the counter, shuffling through some shipping receipts.
When he looked up there she was. "What?" he said. "What'd you
say?"

"I'd like to see Doyle Francis, please. I believe he's still
working here."

"I'll go get him. No, I'll go tell him. Hell. You wait here."

She had her information right; Doyle Francis was in fact still
working at the elevator. In the three months since her husband

had left town, the board of directors had begun to advertise for a new manager, as they had promised Doyle Francis they would, but they hadn't hired a permanent replacement yet because in the intervening days and weeks they had become suspicious of their fellow man. Deeply, excessively suspicious. They had begun to insist on researching each applicant's past—and not just his work experience, as is customary when hiring somebody new, but his ethical and moral and religious history as well. It was as if they had begun to suspect everybody, to believe every man in the world who applied for the manager's job at the elevator wanted only to take their money, to skip town with it. In the end, however, what they really only wanted to ask these men was: "Goddamn it, if we hire you now, how long are you going to be here working for us before you think you have to add to what we pay you, before you turn out to be another son of a bitch like Jack Burdette did? You ought to at least be able to tell us that much."

No one blamed them for this attitude, for this new profound mistrust of others; most of the people in Holt felt similarly. But, because of the board's suspicions, Doyle Francis was still there in April, still waiting for the board to hire someone else so he could relax into retirement again. That afternoon he was still in his old office when Bob Thomas burst in.

"She's here," Bob said. "She wants to see you."

"Who does?"

"Her. That son of a bitch's wife. She's out there in the scale room."

"What does she want?"

"How the hell do I know? She just said she wanted to see you. That's all she said."

"Well," Doyle said. "Show her in, Bob. Or are you scared, if we get too close to her, she might steal your pocketbook or something?"

"By god," Bob said. "I don't trust none of them no more. That's a fact."

"Never mind," Doyle said. "Ask her to come back here. Go on now, try to act like a gentleman for once in your life."

"I don't need to act like no gentleman. Not with her, I don't."

He turned and went back out to get Jessie. She was still standing at the counter.

"He said he'd see you. Come on, I'll show you where he's at."

"Thank you," Jessie said, "but I know where the manager's office is."

"Well don't take too long. Some of us got to work for a living."

Jessie walked around the counter and down the narrow hallway past the toilet and the storage room. She was wearing slacks and a loose green blouse. When she entered, Doyle Francis stood up. He was one of the few men in town then, at least of those connected to the elevator, who still treated her with respect and minimal courtesy. He offered her a wooden chair with armrests.

She sat down heavily, a little carefully—she was still pregnant then, still carrying that little girl of hers that Burdette had left her with; she was in her seventh month. She set her purse on her shortened lap, in front of her stomach.

"Now, then," Doyle said. "What can I do for you, Jessie?"

"I don't want anything. If that's what you think."

"No," he said. "I don't think that. They don't pay me enough to worry about what other people think."

"Well I don't," Jessie said. "I didn't come here to ask for anything. I came here to give you something."

"Oh?" he said. "What is it you want to give me?"

"Not you. The board of directors. The elevator. All these people."

"What is it?"

"Here." She opened her purse and withdrew a legal document. She pushed it across the desk toward him. Doyle picked it up, looked at it.

"Wait a minute," he said. "Hold on now. This is some kind of a deed, isn't it?"

"They said it was legal."

"Who said it was legal? What are you talking about?"

"The people down at the bank. They said I could sign it over to whoever I wanted to, even if Jack wasn't here to cosign it. They said considering the circumstances it would be all right."

"Did they now?" Doyle said. "I'll bet they did too."

He looked at the document again, read it this time. It was a quitclaim deed transferring the title of a house and property over to the board of directors of the Holt County Farmers' Co-op Elevator. Her signature was at the bottom in fresh ink.

"All right, then," he said, "I suppose it is legal. I wouldn't know; I'm not a lawyer. But then I don't suppose anybody around here would protest it very much, would they? Even if it wasn't legal?"

"No. They wouldn't protest it."

Doyle laid the deed down on the desk. He folded his hands over it. He said: "How old are you, Jessie?"

"I'm twenty-seven."

"And you have two boys?"

"Yes."

"How old are they?"

"They've just turned four and three. But why are you asking me these—"

"And you're going to have another one pretty soon, aren't you?"

"In June," she said. "But—"

"Do you believe in hell?" he said. "Is that it?"

She stared back at him.

"Is that why you're doing this? Because, let me tell you, I don't think there is any hell. No, I don't. And I don't think there's any heaven either. We just die, that's all. We just stop breathing after a while and then everybody starts to forget about us and pretty soon they can't even remember what it is we think we did to them."

"I don't know what I believe," she said.

"Then why are you doing this? Will you tell me that?"

"Because," she said.

"Because? That's all. Just because."

She continued to stare back at him, to watch him, her eyes steady and deep brown.

Finally Doyle said: "All right, you're not going to tell me. You don't have to tell me; I think I know anyway. But listen now. Listen: let an old man ask you this. Don't you think you're going to need that house anymore? I mean, if you give it up like you're proposing to do, just where in hell are you and these kids going to live afterwards?"

"That's my concern," she said. "Isn't it?"

"Yes, of course it is, but—"

"And you agree it's legal, don't you?"

"Yes. As far as I can tell."

"So will you please give that piece of paper to the board? You can tell them we'll be out of the house by the first of May."

"But listen," he said. "Damn it, wait a minute now—"

Because Jessie had already stood up. She was already leaving. And Doyle Francis was still leaning toward the chair she had been sitting in. Those good intentions of his were still swimming undelivered in his head and his arms were still resting on that quitclaim deed on his desk. She walked out through the hallway and on outside.

In the scale room Bob Thomas watched her leave. When she had driven away he went in to see Doyle. "Well," he said, "she was here long enough. What'd she want?"

"What?"

"I said, 'What'd she want?' Burdette's wife."

"Nothing. She didn't want anything."

"I don't believe that."

"I don't care what you believe. That woman doesn't want a goddamn thing from any one of us."

"What do you mean she doesn't want anything? She's a Burdette, isn't she?"

"I mean," Doyle Francis said, "get the hell out of here and leave me alone. Goddamn it, Bob, go find something else to do with yourself."

For some of the people in Holt that was enough. I suppose they felt about it a little like Doyle Francis did, that she deserved the magnanimity of their good intentions. Privately, they understood that she was innocent, or at least they knew that she was ignorant. It wasn't her fault, they told themselves; she wasn't involved. They could afford to be nice to her. Anyway, they could refrain from actually wishing her harm.

For others, though, who were more vocal and more active, it still wasn't sufficient. These people argued that the house didn't amount to enough. It didn't matter that it was all that she had, that it was the sum total of her collateral and disposable property. It was merely an old two-bedroom house in the middle of town. It needed tin siding and new shingles; it needed painting. Besides, there was still a fifteen-year lien against it when she signed it over, so that when the board of directors became the fee owners of the house and then sold it at public auction, it didn't even begin to make a dent in that $150,000 that her husband had disappeared with. No, they weren't satisfied. A house wasn't alive and capable of bleeding, like a human was. It wasn't pregnant, like Jessie was.

In any case, by the first of May she and the two boys had moved out of the house as Jessie said they would—they had rented the downstairs apartment in the old Fenner place on Hawthorne Street at the west edge of town—and it was Doyle Francis who helped them move. They used his pickup. Jessie accepted that much assistance from him at least, although after-

●

ward she sent him a freshly baked chocolate cake on a platter, to square things, to keep that balance sheet of hers in the black.

Well, it was a nice enough apartment: they had five rooms—a kitchen, a living room, two small bedrooms, and there was a bathroom with a shower off the kitchen. They also had use of the front porch, a wide old-style porch with a wooden rail around it and with a swing suspended from hooks in the ceiling. From the porch, they could look west diagonally across the street toward open country since that was where Holt ended then, at Hawthorne Street: there was just Harry Smith's pasture west of them, a half-section of native grass in which Harry kept some horses. So it was a good place for her boys to grow up; they would have all that open space available to them across the street.

When they had settled in and after new curtains had been hung over the windows—heavier ones to block any view from the street—Jessie began to take care of the money end of it as well. She began to earn a living. She took a job at the Holt Cafe on Main Street. Six days a week she worked as a waitress, rising each morning to feed TJ and Bobby and to play with them until just before noon when the sitter, an old neighbor lady—Mrs. Nyla Waters, a kindly woman, a widow—came to watch the boys while Jessie worked through the noon rush and the afternoon and the dinner hour, and then returned again each evening about seven o'clock to bathe and put the boys to bed and to read them stories. She often sang to them a little too, before they slept.

And working in this way—being pregnant and having to spend that many hours away from her children—was not the optimum solution to all her problems either, of course, but she didn't have many alternatives. She refused to consider welfare. Accepting Aid to Dependent Children, or even food stamps, was not a part of her schedule of payments—that local balance sheet of hers, I mean—since any public assistance of this kind came from taxes. A portion of that public tax money would have originated, at least theoretically, in Holt County. She knew that.

And she didn't want anything from people in Holt. Not if she hadn't paid for it, she didn't. Doyle Francis was right about that.

But then, toward the end of spring that year, she discovered a way to make the final payment. She began to go out dancing at the Holt Legion on Saturday nights.

But no one would dance with her at first. She came down the stairs that first Saturday night early in May and walked over to the bar, lifted herself onto a barstool, ordered a vodka Collins, and waited. And nothing happened. Maybe it got a little quieter for a moment, but not very much, so she couldn't be certain that she'd even been noticed. She looked lovely too: she had made herself up and had put on a deep blue dress which was loose enough that her stomach showed only a little, as if she was merely in the first months of pregnancy; she was wearing nylons and heels; her brown hair was pulled away from her face in such a way that her eyes appeared to be even larger and darker than they were ordinarily. Sitting there, she waited; no one talked to her; nothing happened; finally she ordered another drink. On either side of her, men on barstools were talking to one another, so she swung around to look at the couples in the nearby booths. They were laughing loudly and rising regularly from the booths to dance. Maybe they looked at her; maybe they didn't—she didn't know. So that first night she sat there at the bar, waiting, for almost two hours. Then she went home.

The second time, that second Saturday—this would have been about the middle of May now—she drank a small glass of straight vodka at home in the kitchen before she went out. Also, she was dressed differently this time. There was more blue makeup over her eyes and she was wearing a dark red dress with a low neckline which showed a good deal of her full breasts, a dress which made no pretense of disguising her pregnancy; it was stretched tight across her stomach and hips. Preparing to go out, she combed her hair close against her cheeks, partially obscuring her face, and then she entered the Legion again, walked down the steps into that noise and intense Saturday night revelry a second time. And as before, she mounted a barstool, ordered a drink, and then she turned around, with that short red dress hiked two inches above the knees of her crossed legs, with a look of expectation, of invitation almost, held permanently on her beautiful face.

Well, it was pathetic in its lack of subtlely. But subtlety and pathos are not qualities which are much appreciated at the Legion on Saturday nights, so she only had to sit there for an hour this second time before Vince Higgims, Jr., asked to her to dance. Vince was one of Holt County's permanent bachelors, a lank, black-haired man, a man considered by many of us to be well-educated in the ways of strong drink and ladies in tight dresses. "Come on, girl," Vince said. "They're playing my song."

They were playing Lefty Frizzell's "I Love You in a Thousand Ways," with its promise of change, the end of blue days—a song with a slow enough tempo to allow Vince, Jr., to work his customary magic. He led Jessie out onto the crowded floor and pulled her close against his belt buckle; then he began to pump her arm, to walk her backward in that rocking two-step while she held that permanent look of invitation on her face and he went on smiling past her hair in obvious satisfaction. They danced several dances that way, including a fast one or two so that Vince could demonstrate his skill at the jitterbug—he twirled her around and performed intricate movements with his hands—then they cooled off again with a slow song.

And that's how it began: innocently enough, I suppose, because unlike some of the others in town, at least Vince Higgims meant Jessie Burdette no harm. I doubt that Vince even had hopes of any postdance payoff. It was merely that he was drunk and that he liked to dance. The same cannot be said about the others, however. These other men were still remembering the grain elevator.

They all began to dance with her. It was as if Vince had broken some taboo, some barrier of accepted behavior, so that now it was not only acceptable to dance with Jack Burdette's pregnant wife, it was required; it was a matter of community honor and restitution. And so, ten or fifteen men took their turns with her that night. They danced her hard around the floor. They swung her violently around; they held her clenched against themselves, forcing their own slack stomachs against her swollen hard one. From that point on they danced every song with her. And all that time Jessie seemed to welcome it, to smile and speak pleasantly to all the men who held her. When it was over, though, when the band finally stopped playing and the lights were turned on once again, she was very pale; she was sweating and her dress looked wrinkled, worn out, stained, as if it had been cheapened. She went home exhausted.

But the local routine was established now—that three-week-long Holt County system of payment was initiated and accepted. And so the third time, that third Saturday night in May, it was just the same—only it was worse. This time the men not only danced with her in the same fierce vindictive manner but they also insisted on buying her drinks. She was wearing that same red dress too, washed and pressed again but showing the additional week of pregnancy. It looked tighter on her now, riper, as if the seams would burst at any moment, while above the deep neckline the blue veins in her full breasts showed clearly. Nevertheless, she danced with every man who asked her. They danced and danced—waltzes, jitterbugs, country two-steps, a kind of local hard-clenched fox-trot—anything and everything the men thought they knew how to do, regardless of the violence and energy it required. And this dancing, if you can call it that, this intense communal jig, stopped only when the band stopped. Then, during those ten minutes of brief rest between sets, they drank. They sat her on a barstool and three or four of them stood around her, telling jokes and buying drinks—taking turns with this too, ordering her double shots of scotch or whiskey or vodka—it didn't matter what the combination or how unlikely the mix—they ordered liquor for her to drink and insisted that she drink it. And she did that too. She accepted it all, seemed to welcome it all, as if she were privately obliged to honor any demand.

Of course by the evening's end she was even more exhausted this time than she had been the previous Saturday night. Also, she was very close to being drunk. When the lights came on at last, when the last man stopped dancing with her, she could barely walk off the dance floor. She was weak on her feet; there was a drunken waver in her step. She didn't say anything, though. Nothing in the way of complaint, I mean. And when that last man thought to ask her if she were coming back again the next week, she said: "You want me to, don't you?"

"Why course," he said. "Don't you know I'll be here? We'll all be here."

"Then I will too," she said.

And she was. Only, by this time, many of the women and at least some of the men in town were growing a little uneasy, a little uncomfortable with this particular form of weekly gambol and amusement. So not everyone showed up the following week, that last Saturday in May. Jessie did, though. It was the last time that she went to the Legion for a long time.

But again it was the same. She was wearing that same red dress, as if it were a uniform now, an essential part of the routine, and there was the same excessive amount of makeup on her face. She was drinking too—it was obvious in fact that she'd been drinking heavily even before she arrived at the Legion. She entered the bar-and-dance room about nine o'clock and didn't even bother this time to lift herself onto a barstool. She merely waited inside the door, with the music and smoke and laughter already at full strength around her. She didn't have to wait long: two or three men discovered her at the same moment and ushered her in.

"What are you drinking?" one of them said.

"Don't you want to dance first?"

"No, let's have a drink. I'm buying."

"All right," she said. "A whiskey sour, then."

"Make it a double," he said.

She drank it fast, as if it were no more than water or lemonade, as though she was no more conscious of what she drank than she was of the banter around her. When she had finished it, she set the glass down and said: "Now who's going to ask me to dance? I thought you boys knew how to dance."

"I'll show you how to dance," one of them said. "Come on."

This was Alden Haines, a man of forty-three who was only recently divorced and who farmed a couple of irrigated circles of corn east of town. He was not a bad man really, but he was still angry at the time about the divorce: his wife had been the one to initiate the legal proceedings. More to the point, he was a shareholder in the Farmers' Co-op Elevator. "See if you can keep up with this," he said.

He took her out onto the dance floor. Pushing roughly through the other couples, he began immediately to swing her about the floor in circles and abrupt spins. Jessie kept up with him, moving him back and forth or circling at the end of his out-stretched arm. Watching her, she seemed almost feverish with intensity, as if she were resolved to test some private limits. When the dance ended, she and Haines were both sweating. The band played a slower song next and Haines pulled her close to himself, clenching his hands behind her back while she held tightly to his neck. He rocked her backward across the floor in time to the slow music. Neither of them talked. When the song ended, someone else cut in, and so it began again, with the same intensity, with

the same feverish resolve. It went on in that way until the end of
the set.

Then the band broke for ten minutes and the local men
bought her drinks again at the bar. While they stood around her,
not speaking to her very much but merely talking and joking
among themselves while still paying close attention to the level
of liquor in her glass, the rest of the people in the Legion that night
were also ordering fresh drinks. The two or three barmaids were
kept busy carrying trays of glasses and bottles out to them in the
booths. Across the room somebody started throwing ice cubes at
one of the barmaids to get her attention. "Stop that," she called.
"I see you—I'll be there in a minute."

Then the ten-minute break was over. The band resumed
their places at the far end of the room and began to play. And
Alden Haines led Jessie out onto the floor again. It was a fast
song, the band's rendition of "That'll Be the Day." He swung
her violently out at the end of his arm—and that was the end
of it. Almost before it had begun, it was finished, completed. I
suppose it was the ice cubes on the floor. Or perhaps during
the break someone had spilled beer or liquor in the dance area.
No one was certain what it was. But in any case, her foot
slipped on something wet and she went down. She tried to
catch herself when she fell but she couldn't; she fell forward,
hard, and didn't get up immediately. Afterward she lay there in
her red dress while the people around her stopped dancing.
She turned onto her side, pulling her legs upward against
herself. Haines leaned over her.

"You all right?" he said. "Can you get up?"

He lifted under her arm, helping her to stand. She was very
pale. She was sweating again now, her face shining like wet chalk
in the dim light. In the center of the dance floor she stood
unsteadily on her feet while Alden Haines held her arm and people
watched. "I think I need to go to the rest room," she said.

"You want me to walk you upstairs?"

"No. I want to be alone."

Later it was obvious that the pains had already begun while she was so still on the dance floor—those who were there remember seeing her eyes focus peculiarly, a kind of brief intermittent stare—but she refused any assistance. She walked off the dance floor by herself, past the bar and up the stairs to the rest room near the front entrance. She went inside, into one of the toilet stalls, and sat down. They waited for her to come back. When she was still there ten minutes later, a couple of women went in to check on her. She was still seated on the toilet, still conscious but quiet and very white. She was bent forward over her knees. There were clots of blood in the toilet. One of the women came outside into the hallway and said they should call the ambulance.

The ambulance got there in five or six minutes. The attendants went in and brought her back out in a wheelchair, tipping it backward to get down the front steps, and then they pushed the chair up a ramp into the ambulance and drove to the hospital. None of that took very long—the hospital is only three or four blocks east of the Legion—but it wouldn't have mattered if it had taken an hour.

When they arrived at the hospital, they wheeled her into the emergency room and Dr. Martin laid her down on a bed and examined her. He lifted her dress and noticed the blood. Then he listened for fetal heart tones. He couldn't hear anything, though: the little girl inside her was already dead. Afterward he said the placenta and uterine walls had separated. When she fell, she had gone immediately into labor, and because its source of oxygen had been cut off, the baby had died within minutes—probably during the time Jessie was still in the rest room. He didn't tell her that, though. He didn't want to upset her: she still had to deliver the baby.

They gave her Pitocin to help stimulate the contractions. But she was in labor for nearly ten hours and there was additional loss of blood and she might have died. But finally she delivered the baby late on Sunday evening.

Afterward they held it up so she could look at it for a moment. The little girl was ashen but otherwise it looked quite normal. Jessie reached up and touched one of its feet. Then they took it away and one of the nurses said: "I'm so sorry, Mrs. Burdette."

So people in Holt thought she would cry then. They thought she would break down at last. I suppose they wanted her to do that. But she didn't. Perhaps she had gone past the point where human tears make any difference in such cases, because instead, she turned her face away and shut her eyes and after a while she went to sleep.

She stayed in the hospital for most of that next week. Mrs. Waters, her neighbor, took it upon herself to care for TJ and Bobby during that period. The old woman brought them in to see their mother as soon as she was able to have company and Jessie talked to them every day and held their hands and brushed the hair off their foreheads. She refused, however, to talk to any of the hospital staff about the little girl she had delivered and she refused absolutely to talk to a local minister when he came to her room to visit her. She preferred to lie quietly, looking out the window. When the week was over, they released her and she went home again, to the old Fenner house on Hawthorne Street. And then in another week she returned to work at the Holt Cafe. In the following months she continued to refill the townspeople's cups with coffee and to bring them steak and potatoes from the kitchen.

And so I don't know what monetary value people place on baby girls in other areas, but here we learned in May that year that $150,000—less the resale value of a two-bedroom house in the middle of town—was a figure that seemed appropriate.

NINE

That was in the spring of 1977. Afterward things in Holt returned to a quiet normalcy. Jessie continued to live at the west edge of town with her sons. The two boys were growing up and she went on working every day at the Holt Cafe and gradually people in town stopped talking about her husband. Of course Charlie Soames was still here. He was still nodding his head and lisping nonsense while he watered the grass or sat on the front porch swing. But in time people grew used to his altered presence, so that it was no longer maddening to see him. They began to forget about his part in the events of that spring. They thought of him now, if they happened to think of him at all, as just an old empty-headed man who lived in town on Cedar Street. Matters in Holt grew quiet and routine once more.

Then in the summer of 1982 another series of events began which ultimately had relevance for this story. These events began with the death of another girl in Holt.

She was a beautiful child. She resembled her mother. She had Nora's rich black hair and white skin, and she was small-boned and bright and neat looking, and she had her mother's blue eyes. But she was like me too, in some ways. She didn't like to stay home. She wanted to be out where there was something happening; she wanted to know things.

So she was a favorite among her friends, and when she was a teenager she was out of the house most of the time, going places, even if it was only to ride up and down Main Street in someone's car. She and her mother were very close, however. And I believe Nora was silently pleased that Toni was unlike herself in that one regard at least, that she was lively and gregarious and had friends, because Nora had very few friends and was often very lonely in Holt. Nora had never liked living here; it was too raw for her; there wasn't the slightest hint of any culture that she could recognize. Consequently she spent much of her time alone, gardening in the backyard, growing roses, and she read a great deal. Then too, she would often drive to Boulder for a weekend, to visit her aging father, Dr. Kramer, the old professor. Afterward she would come back to Holt and appear to be cheerful for a day or two. But it would never last. After eighteen years of marriage we had achieved an unhappy and silent compromise: for Toni's sake we stayed together. We didn't talk about the future and while we were generally kind in our daughter's presence and made a pretense at being contented, we were essentially indifferent to one another. But in the summer of 1982 even that seemed too much to pretend about any longer.

It was the custom in Holt County for graduating high-school seniors to have a keg party out in the country on the night of graduation. Usually some of the parents sponsored the party, thinking it would be better to have adults in attendance to ensure that the kids didn't do anything too crazy, to see to it that when they left in the early hours of the morning someone in the car was sober enough to drive home. Besides the beer, the parents

·

provided a midnight breakfast, enough for everyone, and such an arrangement had always worked satisfactorily. Afterward there would be something eventful for the kids to remember, to mark their passage into adulthood, and no one got hurt.

Toni, our sixteen-year-old daughter, had gone to the party that year. Not that she was graduating yet—she had just finished her sophomore year at the Holt County Union High School—but she was dating a boy who was a senior and so she had gone with him. He was a nice kid. Nora and I both liked him. He was generally a responsible boy and he had treated Toni with affectionate kindness. They had been dating for almost a year. His name was Danny Pohlmeier.

The night of the party Nora and I had gone to sleep as usual, after watching the ten o'clock news. Then about four o'clock the police woke us. It was Dale Willard, the deputy sheriff, who came and knocked on the door. I put my pants on to go downstairs. Willard was standing on the front porch in the dark. I turned the light on. Under the porch light Willard's face looked pasty and tired. "There's been an accident," he said. "You'd better come down to the hospital."

"What's wrong? Is it Toni?"

"It doesn't look very good."

"You mean she's badly hurt?"

Willard didn't say anything.

"Tell me," I said. "Is she badly hurt?"

"You better come down to the hospital. I don't know how to tell you this."

"You mean it's worse than that."

Willard looked at me quickly. "I'm sorry," he said. Then there wasn't anything more to say. He turned and walked off the porch. But he stopped again and turned back. "I'll wait for you in the car. If you want me to."

I stood watching him a moment. He walked on out to the county's blue police car where it was parked at the curb and got in and closed the door quietly and then sat waiting with his hands on the steering wheel, looking straight ahead out through the windshield. I couldn't move yet. It was cool outside on the porch. There was a slight breeze blowing. The stars were very high and clear overhead. *Oh, god.* Finally I went back upstairs to tell Nora.

She was awake, sitting up in the bed in her nightgown. Her hair appeared very black against her nightgown and her pale shoulders. "Who was it?" she said.

"Dale Willard."

"What did he want? Doesn't he have something to do with the police?"

"He's the deputy sheriff."

"What did he want?"

"It's about Toni," I said. "She's at the hospital. He said Toni's been hurt."

"No," Nora said. "Oh no. No."

She didn't say anything more. Her eyes widened and then narrowed, and her lips moved, but there was no other sound now. She seemed to be holding herself from any further display of emotion. She got dressed and we went downstairs.

Outside Dale Willard was still sitting in the county police car in front of our house.

"Do you want to ride with him?" I said. "He's waiting for us." Nora shook her head.

So I walked over to the car and told him we would drive ourselves. We got into our own car and drove to the hospital. The streets were empty and quiet and the houses were all dark, but Dale Willard followed us anyway. I believe he felt responsible for seeing that we got there safely.

At the hospital one of the nurses met us at the back entrance and showed us into a waiting room. Then she left. In a moment Dr. Martin came in and we stood up while he told us about it. One of the other kids in a car driving home from the party half an hour later had discovered them. Toni and the Pohlmeier boy

had left the party together, at about two-thirty, and apparently
he was driving too fast and he had gotten over too far onto the
loose sand at the side of the country road. Then he must have tried
too quickly to correct it—the car had rolled over four or five
times. They couldn't be sure how many times it had rolled over,
but when it had stopped it was in the barrow ditch, upside down.
There was glass everywhere and the roof was smashed down level
with the hood and trunk.

"Where is Toni now?" I said.

Dr. Martin ignored that for the moment. He went on. He said
he thought that Danny Pohlmeier was going to live. There was
a good chance of it, he said. He was a healthy young boy. It was
too soon to tell, though. They were making arrangements to fly
him to Denver.

"Where is Toni?" I said.

Dr. Martin looked at Nora. "We have your daughter in a
room just down the hall here. But I don't think she suffered. It
was too sudden. I feel certain she didn't suffer."

"Where is she? We want to see her."

"I don't think you do."

"Yes," I said. "We want to see her."

He looked at Nora again. She was standing very rigidly,
watching him. "Very well," he said.

I took Nora's arm and we followed Dr. Martin down the
hallway to one of the rooms in the emergency area. Inside on an
examining table there was a small figure with a white sheet pulled
over it.

"We want to be alone now," I said.

Dr. Martin took my hand and pressed it and put his arm
around Nora's shoulders. He was going to say something more but
evidently thought better of it. He went out and shut the door.

After he was gone Nora lifted the sheet. We could see Toni's
poor face then. Her black hair was matted at the side of her head
and her face was swollen and discolored. Her eyes were only

half-shut. Her face had been badly cut up and she had bled from
the nose and mouth. There was dried blood in her nostrils and
there was more blood at the corners of her mouth.

"Oh god," I said. "That's enough, Nora. Put it back now.
Jesus god."

But Nora lifted the sheet so that she could see all of Toni's
body. They had cut her clothes off. Our daughter looked very
small and broken. Nora moved her fingers gently over the bruised
arms and then she walked over to the counter and pulled a
Kleenex from a box and moistened it with her tongue so she could
removed the dried blood from Toni's mouth. She bent and kissed
the forehead and put the sheet back.

After that we went home again. It was beginning to be
daylight now. And later in the morning John Baker, who owned
the mortuary, came to the house and we made the arrangements
for the funeral. A couple of days later Toni was buried in the Holt
County Cemetery northeast of town.

It was a large funeral; all of her friends from school were
there and many of their parents and various townspeople.
There were a great many flowers at the altar of the church.
The minister spoke and there was some music, I remember,
and afterward, at the cemetery, after the brief prayers and
rites, people filed past us to shake our hands while we stood in
the shade under the green awning at the gravesite. For the
funeral John Baker had done what he could with Toni's face,
but it was not recognizable. It was merely the mask of a dead
child, caked with powder and waxen-looking. So we had not
permitted the casket to be opened and we had not allowed
anyone to view her at the mortuary in the evenings before the
funeral. When it was all finished and everyone had driven
away, Nora and I went home again to a house that seemed
utterly quiet. None of the public ceremonies had helped.

*   *   *

But as it turned out Danny Pohlmeier did live, as Dr. Martin said he might. He was in the hospital in Denver for two or three months and then he was in a cast for another half year or so. When he was home again he came to the house one night to talk to us. He sat on the couch and cried into his hands while he told us about it. After he had stopped talking there was nothing more to say. We walked him to the front door and he left. Nora and I did not blame him for what had happened. We did not feel that way about it. He was a nice boy and it was obvious that he felt very badly. Still we never mentioned his name to one another again.

In fact we were hardly speaking at all. It was an awful summer. Nora was quieter and even more withdrawn than she had ever been. She couldn't sleep at night and she had begun to take things to make her sleep. Then she would get up late in the morning with a headache and move silently about the house. In the evenings she would still garden a little, among her roses, pulling weeds and dusting the flowers with insecticide, but she wasn't much interested in her roses anymore and she had begun to wear white gloves whenever she worked outside. They were the same gloves she had worn previously to church and for women's society meetings; now she was using them to protect her hands from the soil in the backyard. It was as though she were afraid of being contaminated by even that much of Holt County. Finally at the end of summer we agreed that it would be better if she left town for a while.

We gave people another reason for her leaving, however. Earlier that spring her father had been forced to retire from teaching at the university and he had decided that he wanted to move to Denver, to be in a larger city. He needed help to make the move. So at the beginning of September, Nora went to Boulder to assist in making the arrangements. We were both relieved that she was going to be gone for a time.

Then she refused to come back. It was at this time that Nora

rented for her father the large apartment on Bannock Street, on
the ground floor of an old Victorian house. It was a roomy place.
It had leaded windows and outside there was ivy growing on the
brick walls, with a black wrought-iron fence separating the house
from the sidewalk and street, and evidently the whole thing suited
the old man so well that he was quite pleased with his daughter
and even told her so. Consequently Nora stayed awhile longer to
help him establish his desk and his books. Then she decided to
stay with him permanently. She took a job at the city library
downtown and returned every evening to cook supper for him.
It was an arrangement they both seemed to like. She wrote me
a letter about it. That was how I learned that she was not coming
back.

I wasn't certain how I felt about this. The truth is, I did not
miss her particularly. It was easier in the house without her there,
without having to watch her every day. But a week or two later,
on a Sunday, I drove to Denver to see them. I took Nora and the
old gentleman out to eat at a restaurant. It was a place they
suggested. There were white linen cloths and linen napkins folded
in cones on the tables and heavy silverware beside the white
plates. There were several wineglasses too. Dr. Kramer ordered
the wine and when the waiter brought the bottle to the table the
old man made a bit of dignified show, sniffing the cork and feeling
it with his papery fingers. He decided the cork was sufficiently
moist and told us it proved that the bottle had been placed on its
side, that the cork hadn't been allowed to dry out. Then the waiter
poured wine into his glass and he tasted that and it seemed that
the wine was satisfactory too. We all had a glass of wine.

So it was a long complicated meal of four or five courses. But
Nora and the old man appeared to enjoy it. I had to admit that
Nora's face looked lovely again; the rigid control she had held on
herself during the summer seemed to have been relaxed and she
looked almost girlish once more. She sat beside her father and was
very attentive to him. They discussed each course as it was

brought by the waiter, sampling the food the other had ordered
and making comparisons. Later we had dessert and coffee. Then
we were finished with dinner and so we drove around in the city
for an hour, across town through the city park and past the zoo
and the museum, and back through the Cherry Creek retail area
toward Broadway and Bannock Street. At the apartment again,
Dr. Kramer decided he would take a short nap.

"Of course," Nora said. "Why don't you rest for a while,
dear."

"But don't let me sleep too long. You know I mustn't sleep
too long."

"No. Just for an hour."

"No more than that."

"I'll wake you in an hour. Then we'll have some tea."

She followed him into the bedroom. Through the opened
door I could see her bending over him, removing his shoes and
covering him with a blanket. They were quite affectionate with
one another; they called one another "dear."

When she came back to the living room I said: "Why don't
we take a walk now? I need some air and I want to work off this
dinner. Maybe we can even talk a little."

It was early evening then. It was in the fall of the year and
the trees standing up in front of the old houses in the neighborhood were just beginning to turn. The apartment they had rented
was in an old established area of Denver. Formerly it must have
been an attractive part of town; there were many large brick
houses, built before the turn of the century, but the houses were
nearly all divided into apartments and the streets were lined with
cars. We walked five or six blocks south along Bannock Street and
then turned west where we could see the mountains, high and
blue-looking out beyond the city, and then north, and then east
again to make a circle. It felt good to be walking. It was pleasantly
cool outside and we saw a number of Hispanic families sitting out
on the big porches of the neighborhood houses, playing music and

drinking beer and talking, while handsome little black-haired kids
played games in the yards or rode bicycles on the sidewalks, and
I thought there was a sense of real life in the neighborhood, of
things happening which would be interesting to know about. But
soon Nora was ready to return to the apartment and her father.
"I should wake him," she said. "If he sleeps too long, he won't
be able to sleep again tonight."

"Let's go back, then. If that's what you want."

"Yes, I do."

We walked a little farther.

"And this *is* what you want, isn't it? You want to stay here
and live with your father? And work at the library?"

"Yes. You wouldn't like it. I know you wouldn't, but I do.
It suits me."

"Well. I hope you'll be happy."

"Oh please. Don't be that way."

"I'm not. I do hope you'll be happy. I mean that."

"Because I tried," she said. "I did try, don't you think I did?"

"Yes. I think you did. I think we both did."

"Thank you for saying so." She touched my arm and then
took her hand away.

"Yes. Well. I miss Toni. I can't help but miss her."

"I know," Nora said. "I miss her too."

Then we arrived at the apartment. We stood on the sidewalk
in front of the iron fence.

"Do you want to come in?" she said.

"No. I don't think so. You go ahead."

"Thank you for dinner."

"Good-bye," I said.

She went on up the steps into the apartment. I stood for a
moment longer watching as the lights were turned on inside. Then
she pulled the curtains shut and I got into the car and drove home,
out of Denver onto the High Plains toward Holt.

*   *   *

After that I was lonely for a while. I do not mean that I missed Nora herself very much, but it was the absence of there being anyone else at all in the house. I suppose after eighteen years, even if it is an unsuccessful marriage, you still miss the sound and presence of someone's being there when you go home. I missed Toni horribly.

Finally I began to eat supper at one of the local restaurants to delay going home, and often I ate at the Holt Cafe. Jessie Burdette was still working there. She looked very attractive in her yellow blouse and dark slacks, with her brown hair pulled back away from her face in combs. She was thirty-one years old then. She was very competent as a waitress, and it was pleasant to see her and to talk to her briefly in the evenings.

So the fall passed in that way. I worked steadily at the newspaper office every day, editing and publishing the *Holt Mercury*, printing whatever was profitable and of interest locally without attempting to do anything that would take much effort, just the routine small-town-weekly-newspaper kind of thing. Then one evening at the Holt Cafe, after I had eaten supper, when Jessie brought the bill to the table I asked her if I could drive her home when she got off work. The evening had turned cool and I knew that she usually walked home.

"I'm sorry," she said. "But I drove this time. I was late leaving the house so I decided to drive."

"Oh. Well maybe another time."

"Yes," she said. "Why don't you ask another time? But do you want anything else? Any dessert?"

"I guess not."

She put the bill on the table and carried the dishes back to the kitchen. I finished my coffee. *Well that was foolish,* I thought. *She doesn't need you bothering her.* I got up and walked over to the register to pay. Jessie was clearing another table. I waited for her, then she came back and rang up the bill and made change and I started to leave.

"But, Pat," she said. "Wait. Would you like to come to the house? I could make some fresh coffee."

"I would, if it's all right."

"I'll be here another hour or so."

"Okay."

"Say about seven-thirty?"

"Okay."

She laughed. "Sure that's okay?"

I grinned back at her. "I'm real quick. I guess I'm out of practice."

"I know you are," she said.

I walked on outside. I thought of taking something to her, some cake or cookies to go with the coffee, but the bakery was closed and only the bars and liquor stores and the 7-11 were open now at this time in the evening. So I went back to the office and worked for an hour and then waited half an hour longer; then I locked up again and drove over to her apartment on Hawthorne Street.

TJ and Bobby were watching television in the front room when I walked up onto the front porch. I could see them through the window. I rang the doorbell and Jessie came to let me in. "This is Mr. Arbuckle," she said. "He owns the newspaper." Her sons looked at me. "Can't you say hello?"

"Hello," they said. Then they turned back to the television.

Jessie led me out to the kitchen. It was clean and bright, with space enough for a large table and four chairs. "Do you want to sit down?" she said. "I'll get the coffee started."

"You have a nice place here," I said.

"It's all right. Anyway, it's not too expensive."

I watched her making the coffee. She had changed clothes since coming home from the cafe; she was wearing a long-sleeved blue pullover now and faded Levi's and her hair looked freshly combed. When the coffee began to perk she sat down across from me at the kitchen table.

I don't know what we talked about that first evening—well yes, I do know. We talked about ourselves, about her childhood in Tulsa, her crippled mother and about her brothers and her father, and I told her a little of growing up in Holt. It was awkward at first. We drank several cups of coffee and at nine-thirty Jessie said, "Excuse me a minute," and went into the front room. She told the boys they had to go to bed now. They turned the television off and came through the kitchen to enter the bathroom. I was still sitting at the table and as they passed through the room they looked suspiciously at me. When the bathroom door was shut I could hear them brushing their teeth and whispering to one another. Then they came out and stood beside the table while Jessie kissed them. "Go to bed now. And no funny stuff. Okay?"

They looked at me once more. "Good night," I said.

"Good night," TJ said. He poked at Bobby.

"What?"

"You're supposed to tell him good night."

"I don't even know who he is."

"Tell him good night anyway."

"Good night," Bobby said. Then he walked out of the kitchen and TJ followed him.

"Oh my," Jessie said. She laughed and made a face. "Such manners."

"It's all right. You've done a terrific job raising them. They're good kids."

"Do you think so?"

"Yes. You have a right to be proud of them."

She reached across the table and touched my hand. "Thank you. You're a nice man. Did you know that?"

"I'm not so nice."

"You seem to be."

Later I stood up and Jessie walked with me to the front door and out onto the porch. We stood looking out across Hawthorne Street toward Harry Smith's horse pasture. There was a half-moon and you could just make out the shapes of soapweed and sage against the dark native grass.

"Thanks for the coffee," I said. I started down the steps.

"Pat."

"Yes?"

"Do you think you'll be eating at the cafe tomorrow?"

"I don't know. Probably."

"Then I probably won't drive my car to work."

"Then I probably will drive mine," I said.

"There," she said. "You see? You're not as much out of practice as you thought."

I laughed. It was the first time I'd laughed in months. "Maybe it'll all come back to me."

"I think it will."

After that it was a wonderful fall and winter. I wasn't lonely anymore, and I think perhaps they were good weeks and months for Jessie too. After that first evening we saw each other nearly every day. When she had finished work at the Holt Cafe I would drive her home to the apartment, and then while the boys watched TV or did schoolwork we would sit in her kitchen and talk. We talked for hours. I had never talked with anyone as much as I did with her, telling her things I had not told anyone before, things which I hadn't known I'd thought until I heard myself saying them to her. It was a new experience for both of us to be unguarded with someone, and as the months passed I began to stay at her apartment later into the night, talking and drinking coffee, and then after the boys were in bed and asleep often we would move back to her bedroom. She was a beautiful woman and very warmhearted and generous in bed, and I looked forward to seeing her every day, to talking to her and being with her. I thought about her constantly.

She had Sundays off and during the week we made plans to do something together with the boys. We took drives out into the country, or drove to another town or went to a movie, and if there had been a rain or if the wind had blown hard we hunted arrowheads in the bare fields of the farmers I knew. In the spring TJ and Bobby each found a number of pieces of flint and a few complete points. We ordered books about Plains Indians and about arrowheads and read them together, and one Sunday we spent an afternoon constructing a glass display case to put the points in. The boys lined it with dark velvet. They were pleased with what they had made and I believe they came to think that I was all right too. I certainly thought they were. They were wonderful little boys and I was crazy about their mother.

There was one day in the summer that we drove to Denver. It was a Sunday in August. We left Holt about noon, driving west across the High Plains past fields of wheat stubble and green corn and the dry pastures, and after a while we began to see the mountains rising up toward us, and then in a couple of hours we were in Denver. We wanted to make an afternoon of it, to take the boys to Wet World where there was a water slide, and afterward we planned to eat at Casa Quintana.

It was about two-thirty when we arrived at Wet World on South Colorado Boulevard. We took our swimming suits and went inside. I bought the tickets at the counter and took the boys back to the men's dressing room while Jessie went to change in the women's. The boys were bashful getting undressed in front of me; they turned their backs and pulled their suits up and draped towels around their necks. When we were ready we went outside and waited for their mother. Then she came out, and my god she looked lovely. Every time I saw her I felt the same way. She was wearing a two-piece suit, with the towel wrapped around her hips. She was naturally brown-skinned and now late in the summer she was a wonderful dark color.

"Good lord," I said.

"What's wrong?"

"Nothing at all."

"What's wrong, though?"

"It's just you. You look beautiful."

We went back to the water-slide area and climbed the flights of stairs to the top. There was a long line of people waiting to go down. You went down through a tube, through fast twists and swoops, sitting on a piece of plastic with a stream of cold water pushing you and at the bottom you shot out into the swimming pool. As people disappeared, going down, you could hear them screaming and hollering. The line kept moving forward, then it was our turn. "Who wants to go first?" I said.

TJ's and Bobby's eyes looked huge. They stood on the platform staring down into the water slide where it made its first turn.

"It's all right," I said. "You'll see."

"Does it hurt?"

"No. You won't get hurt. It's fun."

"Okay," TJ said. "I think I can try it."

I gave the attendant the tickets and he handed us the plastic pieces to sit on. TJ sat down on the plastic and inched himself toward the lip of the platform, then he was over the lip and the stream of water caught him and he went down fast, screaming.

"Next," the attendant said. "Who's next? There's people waiting."

"What do you think, Bobby?" I said.

"Can I try it with you?"

"Yes. Come down with me once, then you'll be all right."

I sat down on the plastic rug and took Bobby on my lap. I winked at Jessie.

"See you boys at the bottom," she said.

I pushed us off the platform, leaning back, holding Bobby with one hand and pushing off with the other; then the water caught us and we went down in a wet rush around the first turn, banking up onto the side and shooting ahead, then more twists and sudden dips and a long fast straight run and a sudden turn up onto the side, the water carrying us and Bobby and I both yelling, and another swoop and then a short run and finally out, flying, still seated on the plastic rug but suspended in air now, and then down into the pool. We went under, I held Bobby around the chest and swam to the surface. When we came up Bobby's eyes were as bright as glass. "How'd you like it?" I said.

"I'm going by myself next time."

We turned to watch for Jessie. But one of the lifeguards standing at the side of the pool motioned us out of the way, so we wouldn't get hit. We swam over to the edge where TJ was. We climbed out and waited. But she didn't come.

"Where's Mom?" TJ said.

"I don't know. She was right behind us."

"What's taking her so long? "

"I don't know. Keep watching."

Then suddenly she came flying out of the tube with a big fat man in yellow trunks just behind her, the two of them sitting briefly on air, his legs around her, and then they sat down into the water in a tremendous splash. They rose to the surface and Jessie swam over to us. "Sorry," the fat man called. "Did I hurt you? I'm sorry." Jessie shook her head and waved at him. She was laughing.

"What happened?" I said.

"Oh," she said. She looked toward the man in yellow trunks; he was climbing up the ladder out of the pool, pulling his trunks up over his fat bottom. "I got stuck about halfway down and I couldn't move."

"Wasn't there any water?"

"Yes, but I lost the piece of plastic. Then that man came down and smacked into me, with his legs around me, and we came down the rest of the way like that."

"Did he hurt you?"

"No it was just funny. And he kept yelling: 'I'm sorry, lady. I'm sorry.' But it wasn't his fault. He *was* awfully big, though."

"Well," I said. "It's a little unorthodox, but you did make a splash."

"I think we did," Jessie said.

"But, Mom," TJ said. "Don't do that again. It's embarrassing."

"I didn't mean to."

"I know. But it's embarrassing."

"Very well. Next time I'll let Pat follow me. Will that be all right?"

"It's certainly all right with me," I said.

"But you should have heard him," Jessie said. " 'I'm sorry, lady. I'm sorry, lady.' God, it was funny."

Jessie began to laugh again. Her sons stood beside her, looking up into her face. I don't think they had ever seen their mother look so amused and animated. She was having a good time. We all were.

We stayed at Wet World for most of the afternoon. Jessie and I went down the slide several more times with the boys, then we got out and dried off and sat at a table watching them. The boys swam and played in the water, diving after a piece of tile, and finally they rode the water slide a few more times. Then we got dressed and walked out to the car. We were very hungry.

It was about five-thirty now. We drove across town to West Colfax, to the shopping center where Casa Quintana was. It was a large Mexican restaurant where the food was satisfactory, but the primary attraction—for little boys—was the entertainment and the decor. The rooms had been plastered to give them the appearance of adobe, as in a Mexican village, and sitting in the rooms you were meant to have the feeling of being in a peasant's house. Most of the rooms looked out at a central square where there was a sunken pool with a clifflike platform above it. Also in one area there was a cave which kids could explore. We walked inside the lobby and stood waiting for half an hour for a table. I gave the hostess our name and told her we wanted a place near the pool, so it took a while for a table to be available. Then there was one and we followed the hostess back through a couple of the rooms to a booth. "Your waitress will be with you in a minute," she said. From where we were sitting we had a clear view of the pool and adobe cliff.

After the waitress had come and we had ordered, some mariachi singers came through the rooms, singing sad songs in Spanish. They were dressed in Mexican costumes with braid and silver and wore big decorated hats. They stopped at our table and sang to Jessie in high voices.

"Ask them to sing something happier," she said.

"I don't know any Spanish songs. Just 'La Cucaracha.' "

"You would," she said. She smiled at the singers. When they were finished we applauded and they went on.

In a little while the waitress brought us our food. There was a small Mexican flag on a stick on the table and if we wanted anything more we could run the flag up and she would see it and come back. When we had finished eating I said: "Don't you boys want some sopapillas now?"

"What are they?"

"They're like pockets. They're made of dough and deep-fried. You can put honey inside them."

"Okay."

•

"Run the flag up, then."

They ran the flag up the stick and the waitress came over to the table.

"These boys want a sopapilla," I said. "So do I."

"Three of them?"

"Do you want one, Jessie?"

"Of course."

"Four of them. With honey."

The waitress cleared our plates and went back to the kitchen to put in the order. While she was gone there was a sudden racket on the cliff above the pool. Two men were arguing with one another, shouting nonsense and pretending to fight; then they each pulled guns and shot tremendously several times, but threw the guns down when they were empty and began to fistfight. They struggled on the lip of the cliff again until one, the bad one, was slugged hard and he fell forward in an arc off the cliff and dove into the pool. Then he climbed out, streaming water, and he and the man above him yelled again at one another while people applauded and whistled. I looked at TJ and Bobby. They were stunned.

"They were just fooling, weren't they?" Bobby said.

"I don't know," I said. "What do you think?"

"There wasn't any blood."

"Wasn't there?"

"I didn't see any blood," Bobby said.

"Well. It looked pretty real to me."

"They were just fooling," TJ said. "You could tell because of the way he dived."

They looked at me solemnly, studying my face. Finally I winked. Then they grinned.

Afterward we ate the sopapillas, leaning over the table, dripping honey onto the plates. Jessie and I ordered coffee while the boys explored the cave in the back room where there was a cache of jewels and other gems studded in the plastered roof.

Later they came back talking excitedly and I paid the bill and we left. It was getting dark outside now and the air was cooler again, as it always is in the evening in Colorado even in the summer.

When we were in the car, TJ leaned forward from the backseat and said without being prompted: "Thank you for taking us to these places today."

"Oh. Well, you're welcome. It was your mother's idea too."

"Thank you, Mom," Bobby said.

"We had a good time, didn't we, honey?"

We went home then. It was almost eleven-thirty by the time we arrived in Holt. On the way TJ and Bobby went to sleep in the backseat while Jessie and I talked quietly and looked out at the flat dark open country and held hands. She slept a little too, leaning against my shoulder. Then she woke again as I slowed down, driving into town. I stopped at their apartment on Hawthorne Street and we walked the boys inside to their bedroom. They were asleep on their feet and I don't think they really woke up. Jessie opened their window and left the door open so there would be a cross draft of air.

When we were back in the living room I said: "I'd better go home now. It's late."

"Are you very tired?"

"I'm tired, but it's been a wonderful day. I think the boys had a good time."

"They did," she said. "But why don't you stay the night? You never have."

"I haven't wanted to cause you any trouble."

"It isn't any trouble. But I suppose you mean the people in town."

"I didn't want them to see me leave in the morning. It seems different if I leave in the night."

"Don't you think they talk about us anyway?"

"Probably."

"What difference can it make, then?"

•

"I don't know. I'm being stupid, I guess."

"You're not being stupid. You're just trying to be nice. Now are you going to take me to bed or not?"

"Well hell," I said. "If you insist."

"I do," she said. "Come to bed, please."

We went back to her bedroom. We felt very close when we were in bed together, and then afterward, before we slept, we looked out the opened window toward the streetlamp while the light played on her face and her shoulders and breasts, and we talked a little, and at last went to sleep with her head on my arm and her dark brown hair, like silk, smooth against my face.

That was in the summer on a Sunday in the middle of August. Then in the fall on a Saturday afternoon in November, Jack Burdette suddenly appeared in Holt once more.

TEN

No one believed it at first. Then suddenly it was true: he was back in town again after eight years. He was driving a red Cadillac and after he had been sitting in the car for an hour on Main Street while people went by in front of him, shopping, paying too little heed to what they saw to understand who it was, Ralph Bird had finally recognized him. And so in the early evening Bud Sealy arrested him and hit him once in the back of the head with a gun and then forced him into the backseat of the police car and drove him around the corner and up the block to the courthouse on Albany Street and put him in jail.

So the local phenomenon was home again. The native son had returned. Only he was behind bars now, locked up in a cell where he couldn't get out, and people were glad that he was. They began to talk about him immediately. They told one another they would get something satisfactory out of Jack Burdette yet.

As for Jessie and me, we heard about it that same evening, on the Saturday of his return. We were in her apartment in the old Fenner house at the edge of town, watching a movie on television

with TJ and Bobby. It was eight o'clock by that time. Jessie had
come home tired from work so we had decided not to go out.
Then the phone rang.

Jessie went out to the kitchen to answer it. When she came
back she said it was for me.

"Who is it?"

"I think it's Bud Sealy."

"What does he want? They were just getting to the good part
in this movie."

"Should I tell him you'll call him back?"

"No. I'll talk to him."

I walked out to the kitchen and picked up the phone. "Bud,
is that you?"

Bud Sealy sounded grim and official. "Listen, Arbuckle," he
said, "I'm going to tell you something first. Then you can tell her
yourself if you want to."

"Tell her what?"

"You're not going to like it. I don't like it much myself."

"What is it?"

"Her husband's back in town."

"What? You mean Burdette's here in Holt?"

"That's right. The son of a bitch come back. You ought to see
him. I got him locked up in jail."

"Jesus Christ. What's he doing back here?"

"Hell if I know. He isn't saying."

There was silence for a moment.

"You still there?" Bud said.

"I'm still here."

"Yeah. Well, I thought you ought to know. There's going to
be a hell of a mess about this."

We hung up then. I stood looking out the kitchen window
into the backyard. It was dark outside and the trees looked black
and still. Then while I stood at the window it all began to race
in my mind. Everything was changed now.

I was still standing at the kitchen window when Jessie came out to see what was taking me so long. She put her arm around my waist. "Is something wrong?" she said.

"Yes. I'm afraid so."

"What is it?"

"Oh Christ," I said, "Jessie."

"What's wrong?"

"Sit down, please. Will you?"

I pulled out a chair for her at the table and sat down beside her. Jessie watched me steadily while I talked. She did not seem to be greatly upset, nor even much at a loss by what I said. And in the months that have passed since that night I have had time to think about it and I believe that it was not so much that she expected him to come back any more than the rest of us did. It was more, I think, that she had managed to achieve a kind of distance and poise of her own, a perspective from which she no longer allowed herself to worry about things she couldn't control. She had been made to suffer so much that spring after he had left, she had had to endure so much that in the end when she had survived it all she was stronger than she had been before and now she saw things differently than the rest of us do. She would no longer permit herself to worry about someone who was supposed to be a thousand miles away—even if he was suddenly back in Holt, a short five-minute drive across town.

Nevertheless when I had finished talking she said she didn't want to see him again. She did not want to have anything more to do with him.

"No. You won't have to see him again," I said.

"And I don't want TJ and Bobby to see him."

"No. But I'll have to. There needs to be something written for the paper about this."

"Will they put him on trial?"

"I don't know. They will want to. It depends on what evidence they still have."

She stared at the white enamel on the kitchen table. After a while she said: "I need to tell TJ and Bobby."

"Yes."

"I better tell them now."

She went back into the front room. She turned the television off and I could hear her talking to them; I could hear the questions they asked and then her quiet voice talking again, reassuring them. I sat at the table thinking about it all.

That was on Saturday night. On Monday I went over to the courthouse to see Jack Burdette. Jessie had called in at work and she had kept the boys home from school. We thought it would be better to let some time pass. The boys were frightened and upset. Nevertheless they went back to school and Jessie went back to work the next day. They were not trying to avoid things indefinitely.

On that Monday afternoon when I got to the courthouse there was a group of men, hangers-on and old local men retired from work, standing around in the parking lot in their adjustable caps and their long-sleeved shirts looking at Burdette's car. The police had moved it from Main Street on Sunday morning and it stood now, long and shiny and red, gleaming in the lot behind the courthouse. Parked beside the cars from town, it looked an affront. The men were talking and gesturing to one another.

"We ought to take a torch and cut this goddamn thing into pieces," one of them said.

"And parcel it out," another said. "The son of a bitch. It was our money."

I went on into the courthouse and down to the sheriff's office. Bud Sealy was sitting behind his desk, slouched back in his chair reading a magazine. He looked tired. I told him I wanted to talk to Burdette.

"Go ahead," Sealy said. "You can try it."

•

"Isn't he talking?"

"Not much. Not since the other night when I brought him in. We had a little talk then."

"But hasn't he said anything?"

"Sure. But nothing you'd want to print."

"I need to try him anyway."

"Of course. You two was friends once, wasn't you? He might talk to you."

I walked back into the jail. I had been there a number of times before, for newspaper stories, and as always the jail smelled sourly rank and oppressive. There were three empty cells, then the last one where Burdette was. I could see him through the bars.

He was lying on a cot which was too short for him so that his feet hung over the end uncomfortably. His feet were bare and calloused and he was still wearing the same wrinkled plaid shirt and dark pants he had worn when he had arrived on Saturday. Over in the corner of the cell there was a small sink and next to it a lidless toilet. He looked very bad, though, so that I don't know that I would have recognized him if I hadn't known in advance who it was. He looked wasted now, massively fat and excessive, sick-looking. I thought in fact that he must be sick; his skin was the yellow color you associate with serious illness and there were deep circles under his eyes. Most of his hair had fallen out in the years he had been gone so that the top of his head shone under the light now, and on his face there was a look of disgust, a kind of unaccustomed cynicism, as if nothing in the world interested him at all anymore.

Then he spoke. And I knew that I would have recognized his voice. "That you, Arbuckle?" he said. "I been laying here wondering if you'd come to see me."

"Yes. I've come to see you. You're news, Jack."

He grinned at me. "You mean this isn't a social call?"

"I need something for the paper."

"Well," he said. "You look about like you always did. Life must agree with you, Arbuckle."

"It does," I said. "But you don't look so well. What's wrong with you? Are you sick?"

"No. Hell. I'm all right. I'll be a whole lot better once I get out of this goddamn place."

"If you do get out."

"Oh, yeah, I'll get out all right. They can't hold me."

"They think they can."

"They can't, though. That's a fact."

"Maybe," I said. "We'll see."

He began to light a cigarette. His movements were slow and ponderous. When he had it lit he tossed the match onto the floor, over into the corner where there was already a pile of cigarette butts and matches. "What'd you want to know anyway? Since you're here."

"It doesn't matter really. Whatever you want to tell me. Except that I don't understand what made you come back. Didn't you like California?"

Now for the first time he sat up. Perhaps the memory of his years on the West Coast still interested him. It was hard to tell; he was so bloated and wasted-looking.

"Arbuckle," he said, "you ever been out there? To California?"

"No."

"You ought to sometime. It's a hell of a place."

"So they say."

"Yeah, it's a hell of a place. Only it's expensive. You can spend a lot of money out there. They got things in California you never even heard of."

"Probably."

"Lots of things."

"Well, you had lots of money," I said. "What happened to it? Did you run out?"

"Sort of," he said. Then, unexpectedly, he began to laugh. "But don't you think they'd let me have some more?"

Apparently the thought of that amused him. His eyes squinted shut and his gut shook; his heaving weight made the cot bounce. "Why not?" he said, going on. "This is my hometown, isn't it? Don't you think they'd let me take some more?"

"No," I said. "I don't think they would." I knew of course that he was joking, that he wasn't stupid, but I didn't care. I had other things on my mind. I told him there were people in Holt who hated him now. "They haven't forgotten anything," I said. "I doubt if they'd give you five cents to leave on. Assuming you were allowed to leave."

"No? I would of thought they'd of forgot by now. But hell, never mind about that. What about you?"

"I don't know what you mean."

"I suppose you hate my guts too."

"Maybe."

"Do you?"

"Look," I said. "You never cared what anyone thought of you before. What difference could that make to you now?"

"You're right," he said. "It don't make no difference." Then his face changed again. There was the show of effort in his eyes, as if he were concentrating. "It's just that I hear you been seeing my wife."

"What?"

"Yeah. That's what I hear. I hear you been seeing my wife. I hear you been seeing Jessie."

"She isn't your wife. Not anymore."

"Oh, yeah. Jessie and me—we're still married."

"You ruined all of that a long time ago. She doesn't want to see you again."

"Sure. We're still married."

"Listen, goddamn it. You leave her alone."

"And I still got my kids here."

"You haven't got anything here. You don't have a goddamn thing in Holt anymore."

"Yes," he said. "I still got my family here. I can count on that much. And this is still my hometown."

"Listen. You must be crazy. You listen to me, goddamn you."

But he didn't listen; instead he began to laugh again. He lay back on the cot with his feet hanging over the end. He was pleased with himself. His heavy sick-looking face smiled out at me from behind the bars. "Anything else you want to know, Arbuckle? Did you get what you needed for your paper?"

"Go to hell," I said.

And that amused him too. It was all amusing. It seemed pointless talking to him anymore. Finally I left.

Then on Tuesday, Arch Withers paid him a call. Over the years Arch Withers had become an embittered man.

After Burdette had disappeared at the end of December in 1976, Withers had gone on serving as president of the Farmer's Co-op Elevator's board of directors and he had finished his term of office, but when he had run for reelection two years later people who owned shares in the elevator had not reelected him. In fact he had been defeated by a large margin, and the loss had affected him deeply. He still farmed north of Holt, but now he didn't come into town very often; instead he sent his wife when he needed something and he never sat drinking coffee at Bradbury's Bakery. He was lonely and isolated, living in a place where he had always felt accepted and admired.

That afternoon when he arrived at the courthouse some of the old men who had been there the day before were there again, standing in the shade, looking out at Burdette's red Cadillac, still talking and gesturing. They watched Withers park his black pickup in the parking lot, then he approached and passed without saying anything to any one of them. When he entered the sheriff's office he demanded that he be allowed to see Jack Burdette. "Let me talk to him," he said.

"Now, Arch," Sealy said. "He don't have any of it left. You know that. Hell, would he of come back if he did?"

"Just let me see him."

"But I can't let you into his cell."

"I don't plan on going into his cell."

"Sure, but if I let you see him, you better not try anything. You hear me? I'll be watching."

"All right. Now where is he?"

So Sealy agreed to let Withers see Jack Burdette. He led Withers back into the jail and then stood guard in the doorway while he began to talk. And it was merely quiet and semirational talk at first, a kind of review of things. But Burdette must have seemed even less interested in what Withers had to say than he had the day before when I had talked to him, and evidently he was considerably less amused. Again he lay stretched out on the sunken too-small cot, lying there heavy and dull, yellow-faced, smoking cigarettes, barely listening while Withers talked on and on. By this time he must have been tired of it all. It was as if he were merely waiting for something. Withers' talk must have seemed to him to involve only some minor misunderstanding between them, an old dispute of no particular significance. Except that it was more than that to Withers, of course. He kept talking, trying to push Burdette into some kind of response. There wasn't any response, though. Burdette simply lay waiting for Withers to cease talking.

So in time Withers grew hot. He began to shout, to curse: "Goddamn you, Burdette. Goddamn you."

And Jack Burdette still seemed utterly uninterested, as if he couldn't be bothered by any of this. Finally he did manage to rouse himself a little, however. He raised his head. "Withers," he said. "I wish you'd shut your goddamn mouth."

"By god——" Withers said.

"I never came back here to hear about your goddamn elevator. Leave me alone. You're starting to get on my nerves."

Arch Withers went a little crazy then. He began to shake the bars, shouting for Sealy to come forward and unlock the cell so he could go inside. "I'll kill the son of a bitch," he shouted. "I'll kill him."

"Sealy," Burdette called. "Get him out of here. I heard enough of this."

"I'll kill him."

"I don't have to listen to this, Sealy."

"Unlock this thing."

"Sealy, you hear me?"

It went on in that way, a violent refrain, until at last Bud Sealy moved down the alleyway toward Withers and tried to lead him away. "Come on, Arch," he said. "Let's go."

"I'll kill him."

"No. You had your say."

"By god—"

"Let's go. Come on now."

Suddenly Withers began to struggle. He fought Bud Sealy in the alleyway of the jail, shouting still, swinging his arms. Sealy shoved him against the bars of the cell, pinning him there, his heavy forearm under Withers' chin, and then he pushed him out of the jail back into the office. Withers stood before him, panting.

"Goddamn it, Arch. What in hell you think you're doing? You want me to arrest you too? I had enough of this."

"He's not even sorry," Withers said.

"What did you expect? Did you think he would be?"

"He don't even care about any of us."

"Listen, go home now, Arch. You're through here. Understand? Go on home."

But Withers seemed too exhausted to move. He appeared to be spent and defeated. It was as if he had been waiting for years for just this moment and now it had meant nothing at all: Burdette

·

wasn't even sorry. Finally Sealy had to take Withers by the sleeve
and walk him out of the office and up the stairs toward the exit.

Outside, next to the courthouse, the local men were still
standing in the shade in the November afternoon. When Withers
appeared in the doorway they wanted to know what had happened. But he wouldn't talk to them. He walked slowly past them,
down the sidewalk. Their heads turned to follow his progress
across the parking lot, past Burdette's Cadillac and on toward his
black pickup. They watched as he climbed into the vehicle and
shut the door.

When he was gone one of them asked: "What happened
down there, Bud?"

"Nothing happened."

"But didn't Withers talk to him?"

"Maybe. But Burdette wasn't listening to him."

"What'd he talk about?"

"What do you think he would talk about?"

"Of course. Well, he's had enough time to think about it
anyway. I bet he made a little speech to him, didn't he?"

Sealy studied him for a moment, studied them all. "Look,"
he said. "You boys better go on home too. There ain't nothing
going to happen here. Go on home and see if the wife's got dinner
yet. I seen enough of you for one day."

After that nothing did happen for a while. For the rest of the
week Burdette stayed in jail, lying on the cot in his cell, waiting,
sleeping much of the time, his plaid shirt and his dark pants
growing daily more rank and wrinkled, while in town along Main
Street people talked endlessly about him, at the tables in the
bakery and across the street in the tavern, and everyone seemed
to know something about it.

But by the end of the week it became clear that something
had been occurring elsewhere. Over in Sterling in the district

attorney's office something significant had been going on: the
wheels of Colorado state law had been turning and what they had
turned up was proof that Burdette was right. He couldn't be held;
the statute of limitations had run out. If he had been out of the
state for five years, and if an additional three years had passed, he
couldn't be prosecuted. He was free to go.

Bob Witkowski, the district attorney, called Bud Sealy on
Friday afternoon to inform him of that fact.

"What?" Sealy said. "What's this? You mean, here that son
of a bitch stole a hundred and fifty thousand dollars from people
and now you're telling me I can't hold him?"

"That's right. That's what it amounts to."

"I don't believe it."

"You'd better believe it. That's the law. And you'll be
breaking it if you keep him. You've already been acting illegally
by locking him up for a week."

"So you're telling me now I have to let him go? That's how
the law reads?"

"That's right. Release him, Bud."

"Well, Jesus Christ Almighty. That son of a bitch. He knew
all along."

Sealy slammed the phone down and stared at the wall.

By nightfall, though, Bud Sealy had gathered his senses and had
decided to act intelligently. To avoid any possibility of interfer-
ence from people in town—there were a number of hotheads in
Holt who might drink enough to think they ought to try something, and it was just the beginning of pheasant season so there
were plenty of shotguns available in the racks behind the seats in
the pickups—he and Dale Willard secretly moved Jack Burdette
out of his cell and drove him out to the county line. It was long
after dark. Sealy had handcuffed Burdette again and had shoved
him into the backseat of the police car behind the protective grille.

Burdette had objected, had cursed and shouted, thinking that Sealy was going to ride him out into the sandhills and kill him. But Sealy had told him to shut up and finally he had. Behind the police car Dale Willard followed in Burdette's red Cadillac.

When they were across the county line they turned off onto a gravel road. Sealy got out and unlocked the back door. "Get out," he said.

"Bud. Now listen."

"Get out, you son of a bitch."

"Bud. Listen to me. You better listen."

"Goddamn you." Sealy withdrew his gun and shoved it under Burdette's chin. "Move."

Burdette slid slowly out of the car and stood up onto the road. He began to rave. "Willard," he said. "Willard, you're here. You know that. You're going to be involved if you let this happen. You know that, Willard."

"Shut up," Sealy said. "We're all involved. Now turn around."

"Willard. Don't let this happen, Willard."

"Unlock him," Sealy said.

Willard removed the handcuffs. He handed them to the sheriff.

"Now," Sealy said, "get the hell out of here, you son of a bitch. And don't you ever come back."

"What?"

"I'm letting you go. You don't know how lucky you are."

"What? So you found out. You can't hold me."

"Something like that."

"I knew you couldn't. I told you—"

"Shut up."

Burdette stared at him.

"And don't you ever come back here again," Sealy said. "You hear me? I'm warning you. Don't you ever come back here. By god, you won't be so lucky the next time."

Jack Burdette looked once more at the sheriff, then again at Willard. He walked over to his car. The engine was still running. He got in and backed the Cadillac onto the highway. Then he honked once, in apparent farewell, a kind of final affront, and roared away. It was not quite midnight then.

The next morning there was a new, even more intense feeling of public outrage in Holt when people discovered that the red Cadillac was gone and that Burdette had been allowed to leave. For a long while that morning groups of men and boys stood in the parking lot at the courthouse where the shiny red car had stood all week. They swore to one another that they would do something yet; they would take some action. But no one could think what it should be.

Meanwhile Bud Sealy sat in his basement office looking out at them from behind his barred window. For several hours they stood there talking impotently and disgusted; finally about noon they began to disperse, to wander home for lunch. After everyone had gone, Sealy called his wife and told her to bring him some coffee and a sandwich. He didn't want to leave, he said; he expected them to come back. And after the noon meal many of them did. They began to talk again, to gesture and swear. In the end, however, nothing happened. It was too late for the local men to do anything about it.

Throughout that morning, though, there had been the fear that something might occur, that someone might be crazy enough to attempt something violent. So about midmorning I suggested to Jessie that we leave town for a couple of days. I had been staying at her apartment all week, out of a sense of protectiveness, and now we decided to take the boys and drive to Denver, to stay in a motel, and drive up into the mountains somewhere. The aspen would have already turned but it would be pleasant in the mountains, I told her, and quiet. She thought that would be a good

•

idea. She called the cafe and told them she wouldn't be coming in. Then we packed and left.

In Denver we took a couple of rooms at a motel on Interstate 70 near Stapleton Airport. There was an indoor swimming pool connected to the motel and the boys swam for awhile, practicing their dives, while Jessie and I watched them and had a drink. There was also a couple from Texas swimming in the pool who said they were on their honeymoon from Nacogdoches. They seemed very young and happy. The girl was plump, with a pretty round-cheeked face, and her husband kept pulling her into the water and squeezing her and whispering into her ear; then she would splash him and laugh and swim away. Later they climbed out and walked back to their motel room, with his arm around her waist, and we didn't see them again.

When TJ and Bobby were finished swimming they took a shower and we ate an early supper in the motel restaurant. Afterward we went out to a movie. We drove across town to a theater in a shopping mall and had popcorn and Cokes and sat in the dark theater watching the screen. But I couldn't keep my mind on the story. They had done what they could to make it seem plausible that an Amish girl would fall in love with a city detective and there were many dramatic scenes and wonderful photography, with a growing sense of something ominous about to happen, but when the violence came it seemed too far away for me to believe it. I sat beside Jessie with my arm over her thin shoulders and watched her face. When we were outside again she and the boys thought it was a good movie. Probably it was. But I couldn't be interested just then in somebody else's unhappiness.

Later that night in bed in the motel room with Bobby and TJ asleep in the room next to ours, I told Jessie some of what I'd been worrying about.

"I know," she said. "But don't you see it'll be all right now? Isn't that what you said? That it was the best thing for him just to leave?"

"That was this morning. When I first heard about it. I felt surer then."

"But nothing's happened to make you change your mind, has it?"

"Not that I know of."

"And there isn't anything we can do about it now, even if there is something?"

"No."

"Then will you please put your arm around me and hold me? It doesn't do any good to worry about it."

"I know."

"And you know I love you."

"I just don't want anything to change."

"Move your arm so I can come closer. There," she said, "isn't that better?"

"Yes. That's much better."

"I thought you'd see reason finally."

We were lying very close together. She felt warm and silky beside me and I began to make love to her then in the dark motel room, with just the dim light showing through the curtains and the sounds of traffic going by outside on the interstate. But everything seemed different now and uncertain. Afterward when we were quiet once more, we lay close together and Jessie went to sleep immediately.

The next morning we got up late and ate breakfast. Then we checked out of the motel. We had decided to spend the day driving over to Boulder and across the mountain to Estes Park. The tourist season was over and skiing hadn't started yet, so it would be quiet and peaceful in the mountains.

When we got to Estes Park in the afternoon we stopped and walked along the streets, looking at Big Thompson River where it went through town and peered in at the shop windows at the pottery and pewter and the expensive brand-name clothes. We bought some locally made chocolate and also some cheese and

fruit and sliced ham and dark bread so we could have an evening
picnic; then we walked back to the car and drove north out of
town along the back way toward Loveland, winding narrowly
down to Glen Haven and Drake, and finally pulled off the highway
at a place where there were picnic tables beside the creek. It was
late in the afternoon then; the canyon was all in shade. We put
our coats on and TJ and Bobby climbed among the rocks beside
the creek and dropped pebbles into the pools and floated pinecones through the narrow rapids, running alongside to follow the
pinecones as they swirled and bobbed on the top of the water.
Then we had supper ready, set out on the picnic table. "Do you
want to call them?" Jessie said.

I called them but they couldn't hear me because of the noise
of the creek. So I walked down to where they were. One of the
pinecones had gotten hung up on a snag and they were poking
at it with a stick. The stick wasn't long enough and they couldn't
quite reach it. "You try," Bobby said.

I took the stick and poked and made a sweeping motion,
but couldn't reach it, and leaned farther out and suddenly lost
my footing so that I stepped down into the water and filled
both shoes. "Jesus," I said. "Christ, that's cold." The boys
giggled and pointed at my feet. I was standing in the water
with my good shoes on. "You bums," I said. "You lousy
bums." I poked the stick again and dislodged the pinecone and
it floated away. Then I stepped back onto the bank and,
suddenly making a grab, took both boys around the head,
wrestling with them against my chest.

"So. You think that's funny, do you? Making a man get his
feet wet? You think that's funny?"

"Yes. We do." They were still giggling.

I squeezed them a little bit. "You think so?"

"Yes."

"Still?"

"Yes."

"All right," I said. I squeezed them one more time. "Now what do you think?"

"We still think it's funny."

"Okay," I said, "I guess it is, then." I hugged them both. Then we walked back to the picnic table. I made a play of taking giant steps and sloshing.

"Mom," TJ shouted when we approached the table. "He fell in the creek."

"Who did?"

"Pat."

"Oh my."

"And he got his shoes wet."

"And he cussed too," Bobby said.

"Did you?" Jessie said.

"Hell, no."

"Yes, he did, Mom."

"Maybe," I said. "But they made me."

"What a mess," Jessie said. "Look at you."

"I know it," I said.

"But you should have seen him, Mom," TJ said. They started laughing again and took turns telling her about it while we sat down to eat.

It was cold and almost dark by the time we finished supper. Still it seemed pleasant there, the four of us, sitting at the same table, with the sound of the creek nearby and the smell of pine and blue spruce all around us. Finally we left. The boys had to go to school the next day and Jessie and I had to go back to work.

We drove home out of the mountains in the dark on Highway 34, down through Loveland and Greeley and on through Fort Morgan and Brush onto the High Plains, past Akron and then into Holt County and finally Holt, with its blue streetlights showing from a distance and then closer, and then the streets all quiet and empty when we drove into town. We walked up the steps into

·

their apartment on the edge of town. We put the boys to bed and went to bed ourselves. We were all exhausted. Jessie and I talked very briefly and went to sleep.

Sometime after midnight I woke again, thinking I'd heard a noise. I lay listening for a minute in the dark. Then I heard it again in the front room. I sat up. Now slowly the doorway filled and it was Jack Burdette. In the faint light from the street corner I could see him standing in the door, massive and dark; he smelled of alcohol and there was something across his arm. I started to get up. Then he found the bedroom switch on the wall and turned the light on. Jessie was suddenly awake too. She sat up.

"Hell," he said. "Don't you two never wear clothes? Jesus Christ, look at you."

Jessie pulled the sheet around her. I started to swing out of bed.

"Wait now," Burdette said. "I'm not ready for you to move yet. Just sit there for a minute."

"What do you want?" I said.

"What do you think I want?"

"There's nothing here for you. You know that."

"Yeah," he said. "Yeah, there is something."

He was leaning against the wall, looking at us. He had cleaned up since Friday night, since he had been released. His eyes were bloodshot, but he was clean-shaven now and he was wearing a maroon shirt and a pair of new-looking tan slacks. The shirt was stretched tight over his gut, and lying across his arm was a shotgun. He motioned with it, pointing it at me.

"I told you I had family here. But you never believed me, did you?"

"That's over," I said.

                              •

"No, it isn't, goddamn it." He was talking very angrily.
"Nothing's over. Is it, Jessie?"

"Yes, it is," she said. "I'm through, Jack. Leave me alone now.
Please. I want you to leave me alone."

"Maybe you just think you're through," he said.

"No. I am."

"I'm not, though. You're what I got left. I'm not through."

"But I want you to leave me alone. Can't you just leave?
You're good at that."

"I'm taking you with me this time. All three of you."

"No," Jessie said. "No, you're not!" She began to cry, looking
fiercely at him. She wrapped the sheet tighter around her.

I stood up. "Goddamn you. Get the hell out of here."

"Shut up," he said. "Shut your mouth."

He stepped away from the wall toward me, leveling the gun
at my face.

"And *you* get up," he said to Jessie. *"You* get dressed now."
He reached down and jerked the sheet away from her; she was
kneeling on the bed with her arms across her breasts. He was still
pointing the shotgun at me. "Do what I say. Get dressed and don't
say anything."

"Jessie."

"I told you," Burdette said.

"Jessie," I said, "don't."

She was still crying. She looked at me and slowly got out of
bed and went over to the closet. She began to get dressed.
Burdette stood watching her. And I hated him now; I hated him.
While he was watching her I made a sudden grab for the shotgun
but he jerked it away and slammed it against my head. Then I was
lying on the wood floor beside the bed, naked, sick to my stomach.
There was blood running from my ear. I stood up wobbly, bracing
myself against the headboard.

"Try that again," he said.

"You son of a bitch. Leave her alone."

·

"Next time I'll kill you."

Jessie had finished dressing now. She was wearing jeans and a blouse and a warm sweater. He told her to pack some extra things to take with her.

"Where's your suitcase?"

"It's under the bed."

"Get it."

"Jack. Don't do this. Please, don't." Her eyes were red and her hair was tangled. "Please."

"Get your suitcase."

She was still standing in front of the closet. She didn't move. Then he shoved the end of the shotgun barrel against my chest, pushing me against the wall.

"Did you hear me?" he said to her. "Start packing."

She knelt beside the bed and pulled the suitcase out, then she stood and walked around the bed to the dresser and removed some clothes, putting them into the suitcase and closing it.

"Now get me some nylons," Burdette said.

"What?"

"Nylons. Stockings."

"Why?"

"Just do it."

She pulled several pairs of nylons out of the drawer and tossed them to him. One of them fell on the floor and he told her to pick it up and hand it to him. "Now back up," he said. "And face that wall."

"What are you going to do?"

"You'll know in a minute."

"Jack. Don't. Please."

"Shut up. Do what I tell you."

Jessie looked at me once more and then turned, moving to the far wall, and stood facing the wallpaper.

"Okay, lover boy," Burdette said. "It's your turn. Make a slipknot in this." He handed me one of the nylons.

"Go to hell."

He raised the shotgun so that it was against my neck. "Don't you think I'd kill you?"

"Yes. I think you would."

"Then make a knot."

I made a slipknot in the legs of Jessie's nylons and gave it back to him.

He tested it, pulling it tighter. "Now turn around."

"You son of a bitch."

"That's right," he said. "Say good-bye."

The shotgun was still against my neck and I turned around. He pulled my arms behind me and slipped the knot over my wrists, making them burn, and then laid the shotgun on the bed and pulled me down so that I was kneeling and tied my feet and knotted the two ends, stretching me backward on my knees. He wrapped another stocking around my head, across my mouth, gagging me, and then made a loop around the leg of the bedstead. Then he pushed me over. I lay on the floor looking up at him, at his tan pants and maroon-shirted stomach. Against the far wall, Jessie had turned around, facing me. She was crying again.

"All right," Burdette said. "We're done here."

He picked up the shotgun from the bed and lifted her suitcase; he took Jessie by the arm and led her out of the bedroom. That was the last I saw of her. She was wearing a warm sweater and she was crying and her brown hair was tangled.

I didn't see any of the rest of it. I could hear only the frightened sounds coming from the boys' bedroom down the hall. TJ and Bobby were awakened and being forced to dress and I could hear the muffled sound of Jessie's voice trying to reassure them, but the boys were both crying, and then there was the harsh deeper sound of Burdette's voice. When they were finished in the bedroom they walked out through the kitchen toward the back door. The door banged shut and in a moment there was the sound of a car starting up on Hawthorne Street; then there was the sound of it driving away. After that there wasn't anything.

For the rest of that Sunday night and for most of Monday I lay in the bedroom on the floor in the old Fenner house. When he left, Burdette had not bothered to turn the light off and during the night I lay on the floor under the bright overhead light. For some reason that bothered me especially, that no one in Holt noticed it burning. But no one did. So I lay for a long time thinking about that and about other things, and then gradually it began to turn day outside, and now whether or not there was a light on in the bedroom of an apartment house at the west edge of town wouldn't make any difference to anyone. Time passed very slowly. Occasionally I managed to sleep a little. Then I would wake again. My ear had stopped bleeding but my feet and hands felt numb and the edges of my mouth hurt from being stretched.

Meanwhile outside I could hear cars going by and I could hear the sound of kids going to school and the barking of someone's dog. Four or five times during the day the phone rang on the wall out in the kitchen. I lay and listened to it ring. Afterward I learned that one of the calls had been Mrs. Walsh, calling from the *Holt Mercury,* and that another had come from the Holt Cafe, from Jessie's boss, wanting to know why she hadn't returned to work. I never learned who made the other calls.

Finally, late on Monday afternoon, I was released. Mrs. Nyla Waters, Jessie's neighbor, had grown worried about seeing my car parked in front of the house all day so she had called Bud Sealy. And so, about five o'clock, Bud Sealy came over to investigate. He came inside and found me tied up in the bedroom. "What in the hell?" he said. "Jesus Christ."

He had to help me get up. While I got dressed I told him what had happened.

Aﾠll of that was three months ago. Since then time has passed as usual. It is the middle of January now, the start of another year, and people in Holt are still talking about the events of last fall. In town Joe Don Williams remains particularly upset about things, since it happened to be his shotgun that Burdette had with him that night. Burdette took it from the rack in Williams's unlocked pickup. The pickup was parked in the alley behind Jenny New-comb's house. So people are talking about that now too.

And in the intervening months the police have begun to send out all-points bulletins again, as they did once before when Burdette disappeared. This time they've charged him with kidnap as well as theft. But they haven't been able to locate him. For as Jessie remarked about him that night in the bedroom: he's good at that. If nothing else, Jack Burdette knows how to disappear.

Sﾠo I am still in Holt County. I am still publishing the weekly newspaper my father turned over to me years ago. And Wanda Jo Evans is still in Pueblo, living on the Front Range, working for the phone company. And Norma Kramer, that fragile black-haired girl I married out of college a long time ago, is living once more with her father in Denver and they seem to be quite happy.

But Jessie? What about her?

Somewhere in this great world I want to believe that she is all right too. I want to believe that she and TJ and Bobby are still alive, even if it is in California with Jack Burdette. No one has heard anything about them since that night, but I want to believe that much and I hope for more.

H

Haruf, Kent

Where You Once Belonged

	DATE DUE		
JAN 2 7 1990 FEB 7 1990			
FEB 2 8 1990			
JUL 1 7 1990			
JUL 2 6 1990			
NOV 3 0 1998			
APR 1 9 1999			